Darcy —————————, ——— ———— buried in Bruce's shoulder.

"Hey, hey, what's wrong, Darce?" he asked.

She shook her head, not knowing what to say.

"Listen, when the semester's over, we'll have the whole summer together. We'll just forget about this whole thing, OK? And start over?"

With a sniff, Darcy lifted her head and tried to read his expression, but it was too dark to see anything except shadow in Bruce's face. She swallowed hard and nodded. "You're right. We'll just forget this whole semester."

But when Josh's face suddenly appeared before her eyes, and she knew the semester could not simply be erased from her mind. It was too late for that.

Bantam Sweet Dreams Romances
Ask your bookseller for the books you have missed

Only Make-Believe

Julia Winfield

BANTAM BOOKS
TORONTO • NEW YORK • LONDON • SYDNEY • AUCKLAND

ONLY MAKE BELIEVE

A Bantam Book / September 1987

*Sweet Dreams and its associated logo are registered trademarks of
Bantam Books, Inc. Registered in U.S. Patent and Trademark
Office and elsewhere.*

Cover photo by Pat Hill.

ISBN 0-553-26418-4

Published simultaneously in the United States and Canada

*Bantam Books are published by Bantam Books, Inc. Its trademark,
consisting of the words "Bantam Books" and the portrayal of a roos-
ter, is registered in U.S. Patent and Trademark Office and in other
countries. Marca Registrada, Bantam Books, Inc., 666 Fifth Avenue,
New York, New York 10103.*

*Reproduced, printed and bound in Great Britain by
Hazell Watson & Viney Limited,
Member of the BPCC Group,
Aylesbury, Bucks*

Only
Make-Believe

Chapter One

Darcy Stevens held her ears as the fifth period bell rang. Nodding her head emphatically at her friend Sandra Grossman, she mouthed, "It was great!" through the clanging noise.

A mob of students surged around them, jostling the girls apart briefly.

Darcy tugged lightly at the arm of her friend's sweater and pulled her down the hall. She picked up the conversation where she had left off. "All we did through the whole Christmas vacation was rent movies and take walks in the snow. Oh, yeah, and we played cards a lot. But my grandparents are just fun to be with, you know. They're still so much in love—even after forty-five years." She shrugged and glanced at her schedule card. "Anyway, who would have thought you could have such a good time just sitting around?"

"You never know, huh?" Sandra grinned at her friend, then looked down at Darcy's schedule. "Social studies with Mr. Webb. You're lucky. Mr. Webb is the most awesome teacher at John Jay." The two paused outside Darcy's classroom, watching critically as other students filed past them into the room.

The redheaded Darcy looked over her shoulder, searching impatiently through the stream of students swirling around them. "Yeah, well, I can live without his outrageous stunts this semester. But Bruce and I worked out our schedules so we could be in this class together. Where is he, anyway?"

Just as she was about to give up and go inside, a tall, broad-shouldered boy in a shetland sweater and khakis rushed up and gave her a quick kiss on the cheek. "Hi, babe," said Bruce McGinnis, smiling at Darcy.

Sandra grinned and hugged her books to herself a little tighter. She was preparing to enter the mob of students and find her own next class. "I've got to go, you guys. See you later." She turned, leaving Darcy and Bruce standing in the doorway, and disappeared into the crowd.

"Where've you been, anyway?" Darcy asked

with a touch of irritation in her voice. She looked into her boyfriend's handsome face and brushed a lock of sun-bleached blond hair from his deep-set brown eyes. She was almost as tall as he was. "I've been waiting for you."

He shook his head impatiently. "I was just coming from my last class, Darce. Jeez. Let's go in." Pulling her by the arm, Bruce led Darcy into Mr. Webb's classroom, and the two made their way toward adjoining seats.

In spite of the reluctance she had expressed to Sandra, Darcy was actually eager for the class to begin. Mr. Webb's "outrageous stunts" were legendary at John Jay High, and they varied from year to year. No one ever knew what project he was going to hand out. One year he had the class create a nonprofit organization and write letters to their state legislature to support it; another year the students had to create a money-hungry, giant corporation and figure out ways for it to maintain a good public image. The only thing they could really count on from Mr. Webb was originality and challenge. So Darcy was more than a little curious as she slid into her seat.

And judging by the excited whispers hissing through the class, it seemed that everyone else shared her nervous anticipation.

Suddenly a hush fell over the room, and a small, mousy-looking man in a rumpled sports jacket and knit tie came in. He was staring intently at a book with dog-eared pages and seemed oblivious to his surroundings. Still absorbed in what he was reading, the man slowly dropped his other books on the desk at the front of the room. He sat down in his chair, running his fingers through his thinning hair as if in wonder at what his eyes beheld. "Wow," he whispered to himself. He shook his head slowly. "Wow," he repeated.

Darcy and Bruce exchanged glances. Mr. Webb had quite a reputation for eccentricity, but this was the first time either of them had seen him in action. It looked as though the semester was going to be every bit as unpredictable as they had anticipated.

"OK!" The intense little man suddenly slammed his book shut and jumped up. He leaned over his desk, his weight on his arms, and surveyed his astonished class with bright, intelligent-looking eyes. "OK! Who can tell me what a partnership is?"

Too stunned to speak, every student in the class sat as if turned to stone. Darcy wished she could think of something to say—something that would make a good impression on

Mr. Webb—but she was as incapable of speaking as the rest.

"OK. OK. Forget it." Waving his hands in a gesture of dismissal, Mr. Webb looked down at his desk, as if expecting to see the answer appear there. After a moment he shuffled through his papers and came up with an enrollment list. He scanned the sheet hurriedly. "Who's Helmes?" he said quickly.

Meek Tracy Helmes looked like a mouse confronted by a snake. A friend sitting next to her jogged her elbow. "Me. I am, Mr. Webb," the startled girl said, timidly raising her hand.

"Right. Good, good." Mr. Webb nodded, as if satisfied. "And Foster. You here?"

Darcy looked around. She didn't know anyone in her grade named Foster. A serious-looking boy with dark, wavy hair and long legs in the back row raised his hand and in a clear, slightly accented voice said, "I'm Josh Foster, sir."

Turning back in her seat, Darcy met a questioning look from Bruce. She shrugged and mouthed, "I don't know."

Apparently satisfied with his scattered attendance check, Mr. Webb walked around to the front of his desk, rubbing his hands together. With a total change in attitude, he spoke softly to a girl in the front row. "May I have a piece of paper, please?"

As if hypnotized, the girl took a sheet of lined notebook paper out of her binder and handed it up to him.

"Thank you." Mr. Webb waved the paper in the air, then gestured widely again. He continued. "OK, just write your names down on this, and I'll check it over later. Let's just get started here and stop wasting time. This is ridiculous."

Leaning across the aisle toward Darcy, Bruce whispered, "This guy is really bizarre."

Her green eyes danced with amusement, and she waved her hand in a silencing gesture, trying not to giggle. In all her eleven years in the Katonah, New York, school system, she had never run across a teacher who promised to make such an adventure of a class.

Mr. Webb now moved to the blackboard and took a piece of chalk from the tray. He wrote the word *partnership* in big block letters and underlined it several times. Turning swiftly to face the class, he repeated his earlier question: "Who can tell me what a partnership is?"

He looked around eagerly, then answered his own question as if he were too impatient to wait. "I'll tell you what a partnership is." He strode back to his desk, opened a dictionary to a marked page, and read: " 'The state of being a partner; an association of partners.' That's helpful, eh? OK, try this: 'Partner: a person associated with another or others in some activity of common interest.' " He slammed the book shut and looked intently at his class.

No one said a word.

"An 'activity of common interest.' I think that's very interesting, don't you? Very intriguing?" He gave a huge grin, and the class stared back at him in silence.

"OK," Mr. Webb continued, "now, this is a social studies class. We will be studying social structures. We do this so that we can better understand the social structures in which we participate. By the way, we'll be talking a lot about economics this semester, because it'll help demonstrate my point—fully." His eyes darted around the class.

"Yes." Mr. Webb clapped his hands and rubbed them together briskly. "So, to show you firsthand—or as close to it as possible—what the most pervasive partnership in our particular—and peculiar—social structure is—" The teacher paused dramatically, staring at the class with his mouth half-open. It was a comical grimace, which gradually widened into a grin—then a laugh.

Darcy and Bruce exchanged another wide-eyed glance, as if asking each other, *What did we get ourselves into?*

Sitting down on the edge of his desk top Mr. Webb shook his head. "You guys are never going to believe what we're going to do this semester. Did you notice, any of you, that this class was restricted in enrollment? Did you notice that there are thirteen girls and thirteen boys?" Mr. Webb looked as if he were ready to burst with glee.

He finally drew a deep breath and announced, "Boys and girls, you are going to—no, scratch that—you are now, all of you, married!"

An audible gasp from twenty-six mouths broke the silence in the classroom. Darcy turned quickly to Bruce, half-pleased, half-horrified. Bruce looked as though he had been hit by a truck.

"Mr. Webb?" A hand wavered uncertainly in the air.

"Yes? Yes?"

A girl in one of the middle rows cleared her throat nervously. "Do we get to, uh, pick?"

Mr. Webb cocked his head to one side.

"Pick? Oh, you mean spouses? No, no, no. It's been my experience that people frequently pick partners for very bizarre reasons." He shrugged, and with a blissful smile at the class said, "So I just did it randomly. And the first happy couple I drew out of the hat was"—he consulted a slip of paper briefly— "Darcy Stevens—"

Darcy waited, an expectant smile on her face as she looked at Bruce.

"And Josh Foster."

Feeling her mouth drop open, Darcy gave voice to an involuntary protest. "You can't *do* that!" She turned frantically around and saw the Foster boy looking at her skeptically from the back row. Blushing furiously, Darcy faced Mr. Webb again. "But, Mr. Webb, you don't understand! Bruce and I—" She broke off, her face crimson.

A few giggles escaped from her classmates. They were all staring at Darcy as if they hoped she could absorb the embarrassment and shock for all of them.

"You can't do that," she repeated weakly, looking down at her desk top.

Mr. Webb smiled serenely. "Sure I can. I'm the teacher." With that, the pent-up nervousness was released, and a flood of laughter swept through the class.

Waving his hand for silence, Mr. Webb continued in a more sympathetic tone. "I know it's a bit of a surprise, but you're more likely to discover the realities of partnership if you have to break ground with someone you don't already know so well. I thought picking names out of a hat was the fairest way to match you all up."

But Darcy was not satisfied. Nor was she giving up. With a defiant look at Bruce she continued, "Well, can we switch, if we want to?"

The teacher shook his head. "Sorry. No way. But remember, this is not for real. You aren't really hitched for life. Nevertheless, I do want you to treat this project as if you were—with a few exceptions," he added with a wry smile. "But I'll get into that later. Let's get through the list of newlyweds first."

The next few minutes were tense ones for the members of Mr. Webb's class. There were plenty of giggles, some stifled groans, and a few more protests. It wasn't until Bruce's name was called, however, that Darcy's simmering anger boiled over again. Bruce's "wife" turned out to be Nancy Piper, a self-satisfied, know-it-all, gossipy girl whom Darcy detested and had dubbed the "Sniper." Shaking her head and rolling her eyes in disgust, Darcy looked

10

at Bruce, expecting to see the same reaction from him. But to her frustration, Bruce looked as though he was too embarrassed by the entire proposal to be upset by Mr. Webb's matchmaking.

"OK, now. OK. OK." Mr. Webb put his list down and jumped down from the desk top. He paced quickly back and forth in front of the class as he spoke.

Darcy was absorbed in feelings of frustration, and she barely heard Mr. Webb as he outlined the project. She was convinced the entire semester would be a disaster, with her married to a total stranger, and Bruce married to that awful Sniper Piper. And she had planned to get her relationship with Bruce back on track that semester. She felt that they had been drifting apart in recent weeks and was determined to set things straight again. Darcy was sure that all they needed to do was spend a little more time together. So, she told herself, there was just no way that she was going to put up with this obstacle to her plans. But it began to look as though she didn't have any choice.

"Finding a home and opening a savings account—you see where the economics comes in," Mr. Webb was saying. "I'll be covering a lot of this in class, relative to the coursework, and I'll expect you to be applying what you learn to your marriages."

"Mr. Webb?"

He turned brightly to a student on his left. "Yes?"

"Is this part of our grade?"

With a shocked laugh, Mr. Webb spread his arms wide. "Part of your grade? My dear class, this *is* your grade! There are *no* tests! You'll have to take notes on three-by-five index cards, write at least a twenty-page report, and make a half-hour presentation at the end of the semester to tell us all how you fared. You will be expected to take the material from class and make it work in your marriages. Don't you see? This is *real life!* We're studying *society!*" His voice rose in pitch and enthusiasm as he ended, and he began absently to run his fingers through his already tousled hair.

Faced with his infectious enthusiasm, Darcy felt herself becoming inspired in spite of her qualms. For a moment she thought that maybe it could be a lot of fun. But then she saw Nancy Piper looking at her with a smirk on her pretty face, and Darcy began to feel frustrated and angry once again.

Through the rest of the class, Darcy sat

fuming, listening with half an ear to Mr. Webb's energetic speech. When the bell finally rang, she grabbed up her books and leaned over to Bruce. "This is the stupidest thing I've ever heard of."

"Oh, come on, Darcy. Lighten up. It won't be so bad."

Irritated beyond endurance, Darcy narrowed her eyes at him and shot back, "Well, it looks as though you're just thrilled to be married to Nancy Piper." She pushed her chair back, stood up, and strode from the room, leaving Bruce watching her.

"Darcy?"

Whirling around, Darcy found herself face to face with Josh Foster. She said grudgingly to him, "Oh, you're Josh, right?"

With an amused smile, Josh declared, "Yes, ma'am. I'm your husband."

"I know. Don't remind me." Darcy looked past Josh down the hall, hoping she might run into Sandra before she had to go to her next class.

The smile disappeared from Josh's face. "I can tell you're not exactly overjoyed by the idea."

Suddenly Darcy realized how insensitive she must have sounded. She felt a flash of remorse, and that made her feel even worse.

13

"I'm—sorry, Josh," she said. "It's just that I have a boyfriend, you know? I—I really expected I'd be married to him, so this 'marriage' of ours doesn't mean anything."

Josh laughed, obviously surprised. "Look, don't worry. I just want to pass this course, OK? I'm not going to attack your virtue or anything."

Staring openmouthed at Josh, Darcy finally burst out laughing. "Attack my virtue? That's very funny." She looked at Josh again, wondering what sort of guy he really was.

He grinned good-humoredly. "Well, I'm glad you think so. Now don't you think we should make some plans? It looks like it's up to us to make time for this marriage of ours. And something tells me it's going to take a lot of work," he added with a wry smile.

Folding her books to her chest, Darcy nodded with a smile. "I guess you're right."

She looked away, suddenly at a loss for words. She wasn't sure how much time she was willing to devote to Josh Foster and her "marriage." "Boy, I don't know about this," she muttered.

"You'll get used to it." Josh was looking at her, his expression unreadable. "Want to think about it and talk to me later?" he asked gently.

A warm rush of gratitude brought a smile

to Darcy's face. She nodded, thinking that perhaps Josh wasn't really so bad. "Sure. Thanks. I'll catch you later."

Then, turning quickly, she edged her way through the packed hallway and made a dash for the cafeteria, dying to find Sandra and tell her what had happened in social studies.

Chapter Two

"OK, newlyweds, let's get the show on the road."

Darcy shifted uncomfortably in her seat and gave a weak smile to Josh, who was sitting next to her. The new seating arrangement had been Mr. Webb's idea. And as far as Darcy was concerned, it was just one more thorn in her side. But Josh seemed to understand. At least he was giving her a lot of space, which was more than could be said for some of the couples. Some heated demands for divorce had already been voiced in the classroom.

With a resigned sigh, Darcy geared herself up for Mr. Webb's onslaught. What she really wanted to do, though, was think about her plans for the weekend. She would be spending Friday night at Sandra's house, and then she'd be joining Bruce for most of Saturday and Sunday.

"Now, I'm going to play the part of the great democratizer and start you all out at the same level. Where you go from there," their fiery teacher was saying with a wry grin, "is up to you. Now—"

As if on cue, all the students bent forward over their notebooks, pens poised, waiting for the vital statistics that would determine their lives for the rest of the semester.

"Each couple will start out with savings of fifteen thousand dollars, which is a lot more than most couples have at the outset, believe me. But, after all, I don't want to be too hard on you. And salaries will be four hundred dollars a week—that's takehome—for men, and three hundred and fifty dollars a week for the women."

"Mr. Webb!" Darcy's hand shot up before she realized what she was doing.

He turned to her with an inquisitive smile.

Darcy could feel the beginnings of a blush suffuse her face. But she was determined to speak, and she challenged her teacher. "Why are women getting less than men, Mr. Webb? That's not exactly fair."

With a gentle nod, Mr. Webb leaned back against his desk and folded his arms. "No, it isn't, I'm afraid. And I don't like it one bit. But such is our society. Women are paid less than men for comparable and even for more demanding or skilled jobs. But there are some political movements afoot. Well, I hope we'll learn something about our society this way."

Darcy could feel his eyes boring into hers; she felt he was testing her, and she wasn't sure what she was supposed to do to pass the test. "Maybe I should write to my congressman," she said carefully. "As long as I'm old enough to get married, I'm old enough to vote."

Mr. Webb let out a hoot of laughter. "Well put! Darcy Foster, isn't it?"

She tilted her head back defiantly. "I've decided to keep my maiden name. Darcy Stevens."

There was a ripple of whispers around her, as well as a few scattered claps. Darcy knew she was blushing again, even though she felt she was in the right. Bruce, one seat ahead and to the right, turned and stared at her with an astonished look on his face. She didn't like having him look at her that way, but she continued to meet Mr. Webb's appraising look. Only when she felt a nudge at her elbow did Darcy turn; Josh gave her a supportive nod. She grinned.

"OK, Ms. Stevens. As I was saying," Mr. Webb continued, smiling at the class at large, "those are the salaries. You may decide that both of you would like to work, in which case your combined weekly salary will be seven hundred and fifty dollars. Or only one of you may choose to work. That's totally up to you. But whatever you decide, you are required to manage the money you have. And how to do that is a matter of research and experimentation—"

As Mr. Webb continued outlining the objectives of the project, Darcy took haphazard notes. She was actually a little surprised at her outspokenness; she had never had any strong political views one way or another. But she supposed that was because, so far, nothing in her life had ever been really hard. Growing up in a family who thought she was smart and talented and having a boyfriend who told her she was pretty had made things quite easy for her—until then, she mused.

By the end of the class, she had filled several pages with scrawled notes—both from Mr. Webb's lecture and from her own meandering thoughts—and she turned to Josh to discuss their plan of action.

As he was bending over his notebook, she had a chance to look at him more carefully.

Working with a total stranger is a drag, she thought, *but maybe he'll turn out to be bearable.* His face wasn't really so bad. His hair was the ordinary brown most people had, but it was thick and wavy, and he had a nice face—with a strong, straight nose and high cheekbones. His long legs stuck out in front of him under the desk; he seemed perfectly at ease and sure of himself, considering the fact that he was in a totally new school. As he looked up finally and met her appraising look, Darcy felt herself begin to blush again.

"Uh, maybe we should—well, get together and work on this a little," she stammered, standing up.

"Sure. Where's a good place for you?" Josh started to pile up his books as he glanced up at her. "How about my house?"

"No!" Darcy realized her tone was too abrupt, and she blushed again hotly. Why was she always blushing around him? she wondered angrily. "It's just that, well, wouldn't the public library be a good place? After all, they've got reference books and newspapers and stuff. And—uh, Bruce wouldn't like it if I went to your house," she finished lamely.

He shrugged. "OK with me. Why don't we go straight from school? I can drive you in my car."

"No!" Darcy had nearly shouted again, and she looked around the room quickly for Bruce. "I'll get a ride with my boyfriend," she said, stressing the last word slightly. "He always drives me after school."

"OK, OK!" Josh's softly lilting speech was mystifying, and he gave her a look that seemed half-amused, half-puzzled. "Forgive me for suggesting anything so improper. I forgot."

Darcy stared at him. She couldn't tell if he was being sarcastic or just trying to be funny. But he continued to gaze calmly at her, and she decided to stop worrying about it.

"All right," she said, smiling. "I'll see you at three in the reference section. There are some big tables and really comfortable chairs there. I know Bruce will come, too, to work."

"With his 'wife'? What's her name?"

Darcy clenched her jaw involuntarily. "Nancy."

With a soft laugh, Josh gave her a light, playful punch on the shoulder. "Hey, relax. This is only make-believe, remember?"

"What do you mean, you can't drive me to the library? I thought you would want to come with me and do some work over there."

Darcy put her hand on Bruce's muscular arm and turned him around to face her. The last bell of the day had sounded, and they were standing at their adjoining lockers.

He sighed. "Darcy, I'm sorry. But Nancy and I are going to work at her house. I didn't think you'd need a ride today."

"Why?" Shaking her head, Darcy laughed in disbelief. "We ride together every day. Why should that change?"

"I don't know, I just thought you'd probably have your plans, and I'd have mine." Bruce took her wrist and shook her hand playfully from side to side. "Hey, come on, Darcy. Smile?"

In spite of herself, Darcy smiled into Bruce's handsome face. She could never resist his smile or his thick-lashed brown eyes.

He leaned forward and kissed her.

"Now look," he said, his hands warm on her cheeks as he cupped her face. "Nothing's changed except that we're not riding home together. You know this project is going to take up most of our after-school time, so we've just got to work around it. All right? You're still my girlfriend—nothing is going to change that."

Darcy nodded, her eyes lowered. "Sorry, I guess I was just looking forward to finally spending a little time with you, that's all. I mean, we've hardly even seen each other since Christmas vacation."

Darcy gazed into her boyfriend's eyes, searching for—she wasn't sure what. But even before Christmas she had been feeling that they were losing contact with each other, and now she was getting worried. For years they had been practically like Siamese twins.

"Oh, Bruce! Bruce, wait up!"

Glancing over her shoulder, Darcy saw Nancy Piper running toward them. She unconsciously moved closer to Bruce and linked her arm through his.

"Bruce—there you are. I've been looking all over for you. Oh. Hi, Darcy."

Nancy's smile was so phony, Darcy thought. In fact, there was something about Nancy's entire presence that just made her mad. "Hi," she said grudgingly.

"Hi, Nancy. Uh—excuse me, Darce—" Bruce released his arm from Darcy's. "I've got to go, babe. I'll call you later, OK?"

She nodded, glaring at Nancy. The Sniper flashed her another fake smile.

"Listen, Bruce," Nancy began in a silken voice, taking him by the arm and leading him away, as she gave Darcy a meaningful look over her shoulder, "I've been thinking . . ."

Darcy stood rigid, watching their retreating figures until they rounded a corner in the hallway. With a silent wish that Nancy would metamorphose into a lizard, she slammed her locker shut and began to rummage in her purse for bus fare.

Angrily stomping the snow off her boots as she entered the library foyer, Darcy caught her breath in the sudden warmth. Taking the bus and walking two blocks through the slush from the bus stop was definitely not her idea of a good time. She looked around for a moment at the familiar clutter of signs, notices, and business cards tacked up all over the cork-board walls and wished for the twentieth time that she didn't have to be there. But she yanked down the zipper of her parka, determined to give it a try. With a cry of disgust, she found she had jammed the zipper. "Oh, for crying out loud. Come on."

Fuming with exasperation, Darcy pushed open the library door and paused for a moment, searching for Josh Foster among the tables. In a moment she spied his head of brown hair bent over an open newspaper. He was making marks with a pen, pausing briefly now and then. She stood and watched him for a moment. Then, as if he felt her eyes upon him, he looked up, directly at her.

Blushing again, Darcy hurried forward, a frown darkening her face as she considered spending the afternoon at the library with Josh while Bruce had been lured to the Sniper's house.

"Hello. Something wrong?" Josh asked, standing up as she approached. He smiled, with a polite, slightly quizzical look on his face.

"No!" Sitting down with a loud sigh, Darcy finally wrenched her zipper free. "This just isn't my day, that's all."

As he sat back down, Josh turned to his newspaper again. In his quiet, lilting voice he asked, "Because you have to spend the afternoon here with me?"

Darcy felt her face grow hot again, and there was a sinking sensation in her stomach that reminded her of the bad way she felt whenever she got bad news. She stammered, unsettled by the fact that he seemed to be able to read her mind. "No—I'm . . ." Trailing off, she looked at Josh's serious face, which was still turned toward the paper.

"Sorry, Josh. You must think I'm the most awful person in the world." She sighed and, without thinking, put her hand on his arm.

Josh glanced at the man's signet ring on Darcy's index finger and turned to her with a wide, endearing smile. "Hey, look, I understand. Really. Don't worry about it." He looked away, as if suddenly remembering something. "I know what it's like to be somewhere you don't want to be."

"What do you mean?" Darcy's curiosity was aroused.

He shrugged. "I wasn't crazy about the idea of moving here to New York." Then an almost imperceptible change came over his face, and when he spoke again, his soft, lilting speech turned into a strong southern drawl. "You see, ma'am, I'm from North Carolina, originally."

A grin of delight spread over Darcy's face; so that explained his accent! And in the last few moments he had somehow made himself *look* more Southern, although she couldn't tell how exactly. Maybe it was the way his eyes squinted slightly or his head tilted back, but as if by magic, he was now the perfect picture of a southern gentleman enjoying his ease on a sultry afternoon. She laughed, imagining him in a white linen suit with a mint julep in one hand. "Well, I guess it's a bit cooler here than you're used to, huh?"

Josh snorted. "Cooler? Why, ma'am, it's

downright Icelandic in these parts." His easy smile returned, and he sat back in his chair, shaking his head. "Anyway," he continued, his thick accent once more suppressed, "it's taking me some time to adjust, that's all."

It struck Darcy suddenly that she had done almost everything possible to make him feel uncomfortable. She'd been dragging her heels every step of the way so far and making it very clear how much she preferred to be with someone else. But rather than have him think that her change in attitude was due to pity, she decided simply to be more cooperative from then on, without making a big deal of it.

She scooted her chair closer to the table. "Well, since you've just moved to town, I guess I have, too, honey!" A playful smile lit her face as she pulled the newspaper from Josh's hands. "So let's find a house. Maybe something in the Red Lakes area."

"Whoa! Wait a minute," Josh said, suddenly serious. He pulled the paper back in front of him and folded over some of the pages he had been marking. "I may be new around here, but I do know that Red Lakes is way too expensive for us newlyweds. Actually, I decided we should look for an apartment to begin with. Then maybe later we can afford a down payment on a house."

Feeling her mouth drop open, Darcy quickly snapped it shut in order to say, "What? *You* decided? What about partnership, huh? Isn't that what this assignment is supposed to be all about?"

"I—" Josh looked genuinely surprised, then he held his hands up in a gesture of apology. "You're right," he said with a smile. "I guess I should have consulted you first."

"Well, sure you should have." Darcy sat back and folded her arms, making a halfhearted attempt to keep a straight face. "But as long as we get it straight from here on in: *I'm* wearing the pants in *this* family."

Josh suppressed a grin as he looked down at her legs. "Um, actually, you're wearing a skirt, Darcy."

"OK, OK. You wear the pants, and I'll wear the skirts, but we make decisions together, all right?"

With a nod, Josh agreed.

"OK, so let's not look in the Red Lakes area, but I'm sure we can find a *house* somewhere in our price range." Darcy was suddenly eager to make some real progress.

Josh let his breath out slowly. "Darcy, we can't afford a house. Period."

"Who says?"

"Look, we've got fifteen thousand dollars. Right?"

Darcy nodded.

"So, look at all the stuff we have to get." Cocking his head to one side, Josh began counting off on his fingers. "One, someplace to live; two, completely furnish whatever we come up with; three, a car; four, insurance; five, pay bills; six, buy groceries every week; seven, have something left over for savings; eight, have a little put away for an emergency."

Darcy was impressed, and she said so. "But if we have to pay rent, that money is just gone. If we buy a house, at least it's an investment—it's ours."

"Hmm. I didn't think of it that way." Josh pressed his lips together. "But, look, I just went through this whole thing with my folks when they were looking for a place for us up here. If we took, say, five thousand dollars for a down payment—and that's nothing—we'd have a mortgage so high, we couldn't afford the monthly payments."

"Oh, come on, Josh, how much can it be?"

He raised his eyebrows. "On a sixty-thousand-dollar house, which is probably the cheapest you can get around here—try seven or eight hundred dollars a month."

"How do you know all this?"

Shrugging, Josh said, "As I said, my parents just bought a house in this town."

Darcy did some fast arithmetic. "But if we both work, then that leaves us—two thousand two hundred dollars a month."

"Yeah, but if we rent a place like this one" —Josh pointed to an ad he had circled—"we'd have two thousand five hundred and fifty dollars a month, and we wouldn't have to be responsible for stuff like—I don't know—the oil burner. Things like that. You know, things that can just go on the blink for no reason. With an apartment, it's the landlord's hassle, not yours."

With pencil in hand, Darcy quickly scanned the list of available apartments. But she still thought she'd really rather live in a house. "Yeah, but if we buy a house, we build equity."

"Equity? I don't really know what that means." Josh now looked impressed with Darcy.

But she blushed—the redhead's curse, her mother always said. "I, uh—" she stammered, and then with a rush, said, "I don't really know, either. I just heard it on a real estate commercial."

The two looked at each other for a brief,

surprised moment of silence. Then they both burst into laughter.

"I guess this is just what Mr. Webb had in mind, huh?" Josh asked, leaning back and smiling at his partner.

Darcy felt a tiny jolt of surprise as she met his gaze. She hadn't really looked closely before, but he had the most unusual eyes she had ever seen. They were deep blue with a rim of brown on the outer edge of the iris. She suddenly realized he would be attracting a lot of notice once the girls at John Jay got a good look at those eyes.

She shook her head, and as she did so, she saw on the wall clock that it was after four-thirty. "Oh, no! I didn't know it was so late." She started piling her books on top of one another.

Josh sat up and pulled the paper toward him, his face expressionless again. "Can you work this weekend? I've got all tomorrow and Sunday free."

"Oh." Darcy shook her head. "Sorry. I've got plans with Bruce."

He shrugged. "Sure. No problem. Can I drive you home? Or is my car still off limits?"

Darcy put her books down and turned to Josh. "Now what's *that* supposed to mean?

Of course I'd love a ride, but I'm spending the night at Sandra's house. She's my best friend."

Again he shrugged. "So I'll drop you off at Sandra's house. Let's go."

Darcy stared at him for a moment. He acted a little odd sometimes, she thought. But she suddenly realized it didn't matter. He was nice enough, and after all, they were only working on a class project together. It wasn't as if they were really married or anything.

Chapter Three

"What's in this stuff, anyway? It smells like rotten milk," Darcy muttered. She looked at her reflection in the mirror and rubbed another dab of the slimy substance on her forehead. Then she shifted her position where she was perched on the counter in Sandra's bathroom.

Sandra shrugged. "I don't know, but it's supposed to give you a flawless complexion. 'Porcelain Cream,'" she read from the jar. "'A delicate hydrating masque to gently cleanse and tone the skin. Developed in Geneva, Switzerland.'"

"Oh, la-di-da!" Darcy said and laughed.

Her friend scooped out a blob and smeared it across one cheekbone. "Just so it works. I don't care if the main ingredient is brains," Sandra declared with a grim smile.

"Actually," said Darcy, "I heard that that's exactly what it is. Brains really work miracles on your pores." She carefully wiped some of the goo from the edge of her lower lip.

"Well, I don't know why you need it. You and your perfect skin." Sandra glared at the reflection of her friend in the mirror.

Darcy chuckled. "Hey, I can't help it—I was born that way, OK? I'm just glad most of my freckles finally faded away," she added.

"Yeah, you used to be one big freckle when you were little."

With a cross between a laugh and a groan, Darcy gasped, "Please! Don't remind me. It brings back all those memories of being called 'carrot top' and 'freckle face.' Oh, hey. This stuff is starting to feel tight. I hope I don't regret this," she added, shooting Sandra a dirty look.

"Hmm. That means it's working." Sandra's voice was beginning to sound funny, a result of not being able to move her mouth when she spoke. "So what's that guy Josh like, anyway? The silent type, eh? The grapevine knows absolutely zero about him."

"Uhm. Huh-uh." Darcy was having trouble talking, too. She paused to think before she went on, staring into her own green eyes in the mirror. That made her think of how unusual Josh's eyes were. "You've got to get to know him, I guess. He's got—nice eyes."

"Oh, yeah? And under what circumstances were you gazing into his eyes, hmm?" Sandra asked, a mischievous gleam in her eyes. She sat down on the floor.

Darcy threw a cotton ball at her friend. "Come on. He was sitting there talking to me, OK? I couldn't help looking at his eyes. You and your dirty mind. Oh, it's getting hard to move my mouth. Besides," she added, struggling to keep her face from stiffening, "I have a boyfriend, remember?"

Sandra tried to smile but couldn't. "Maybe, but don't forget you also have a 'husband.' " She leaned back against the wall and put her feet up on the counter. "Anyway, what's he really like? And why does he have that funny accent? Where is he from, anyway?"

"Sandra, gross. You've practically got your smelly feet on my toothbrush." Darcy reached over to rescue her toothbrush from Sandra's bare toes. She didn't feel like answering Sandra's question and was trying to change the subject.

"Oh, big deal." Shifting her feet slightly, Sandra continued her third degree. "What did you guys talk about?" She grinned, cracking the caking mask on her face. "You going to have any kids?"

"Oh, cut it out!"

"It's such a typical Webb assignment, but if I had been in the class, I would have just died. I mean, it's so embarrassing." Sandra stood up and glanced into the mirror. "What time is it, anyway? If you leave this stuff on your face for more than ten minutes, it never comes off."

Darcy let out a shriek that turned into a giggle. She jumped down. "Sandra! Here, give me that washcloth!"

For the next few moments, the girls were busy wiping the hardened goo from their faces, and the subject of Josh Foster was forgotten. But only temporarily.

"So, you still haven't answered my question, Darcy. What's he like?"

Darcy released a huffy breath of exasperation. "Will you come on! He's just basically a nice guy—from North Carolina. That's all. Period. End of subject. Let's not talk about him anymore. You're beginning to sound obsessed."

Even though she didn't want to talk about Josh, Darcy was still thinking about him. And the fact that she was thinking about Josh Foster worried her. *Why should he be on my mind so much?* she wondered. *I should be thinking about Bruce. But then, it's only natural,* she reassured herself the next moment. *We are working on a big project together, after all.*

"Listen, I'm going to call Bruce, OK?" she announced, a hint of irritation in her voice.

"Fine," replied Sandra coolly. She picked up a hairbrush and began pulling it through her dark curls. "Use the one in my parents' room, OK?" she added.

Darcy tapped her fingers on the bedside table as she listened to the ringing on the other end of the phone. "Come on, Bruce. Answer!" she was muttering just as he picked up the line.

"Hello?"

"Hi, it's me." Darcy wrapped the coils of the phone cord around her index finger and stared absently at the lamp on the bedside table.

"Hey, how're you doing, Darce?" He went on before she could answer. "You're at Sandra's, right?"

Darcy unwrapped the cord from her finger and wrapped it up again. "Yeah, why?"

"Well, so you'll be there most of tomorrow, I guess. I'm glad, that's all."

She quickly sat up and shook her hand

free of the cord. "What's that supposed to mean? I'm not going to be here most of tomorrow because I'll be with you."

There was a brief pause on the other end of the line. "But—we didn't make any plans, did we? I mean, did I forget something?" Bruce sounded upset.

Suddenly Darcy found herself close to tears, and it surprised her. "But, Bruce—I mean, I just figured we would." She swallowed hard. "Well, don't you *want* to see me tomorrow?"

There was another pause, this time a longer one. "Well, sure. I—I mean, you know I do. But I'm sorry, Darcy, I can't. I'm working on this project all day tomorrow with Nancy Piper."

"Bruce! Why did you go ahead and make plans like that?" Every time he mentioned Nancy's name it had an unpleasant effect on Darcy. She was suddenly very annoyed. "We've hardly even seen each other since before Christmas vacation, and now you're going to be busy all Saturday?"

Bruce's voice was very quiet and gentle when he answered. "I'm sorry, Darcy. I just wasn't thinking—I'm sorry." He paused again. "How about Sunday, though? Just you and me. We'll do something special, OK?"

Darcy's anger melted in the warmth of

Bruce's tender voice. "I can never resist you, you big jerk," she said, teasingly. "What should we do?"

"Hmm. That will be my surprise, OK? I'll pick you up at lunchtime. Will that be all right?"

Darcy had to smile. "That's perfect. I love you," she added softly.

"I love you, too, babe. Bye."

For the rest of the evening, Darcy and Sandra watched TV and talked. When they took a break to make a bowl of popcorn, Darcy told Sandra about Bruce's surprise date.

"I think that's one of the most incredibly romantic things I ever heard of." Sandra sighed. "It figures, you would be the one to end up with Bruce McGinnis. I always knew, even when he used to pull your hair in third grade, that he really liked you."

Darcy nodded with a shy smile. "I guess he is pretty incredible," she agreed.

But she still felt hurt that he had tossed away their whole Saturday. She sighed, wondering whether the social studies project wasn't going to create more problems than she had bargained for.

She shook herself. "Come on, the movie of the week's going to start in a minute."

*   *   *

On Saturday morning Darcy's mother picked her up at Sandra's house. The two of them went shopping at the mall for a few hours, and then picked up some groceries at the supermarket. Stopping at her mom's bank reminded Darcy of her project, and she picked up some brochures on savings accounts and investment plans. She thought it was pretty clever of her to think of doing it, and she looked forward to showing Josh how farsighted she had been.

But thinking about her project with Josh naturally made her think of Bruce spending the day with the Sniper. And she also couldn't help thinking that, aside from picking up a few brochures, she couldn't even get any work done on her own project. She had told Josh she would be busy with Bruce all weekend, so they hadn't made plans. And there was no way she was going to call him and admit she had been stood up. Suddenly the pamphlets from the bank looked stupid and boring to her.

So Saturday was a washout as far as Darcy was concerned. She baked two loaves of bread and then finished a novel she had been reading, nibbling away at half a loaf as she sat at the kitchen table with the book propped up in front of her.

At last, Sunday arrived. When Darcy heard Bruce's car in the driveway, she gave her thick hair a final stroke with her hairbrush and examined her reflection critically. She was wearing one of Bruce's favorite outfits: a black, green, and white kilt and a green blouse that set off the red deep highlights of her hair.

But Bruce's face fell when he saw her. "You look great," he said uncertainly, as he kissed her cheek. "But you'll have to change."

"But why?" Darcy asked, feeling hurt in spite of his compliment.

"Because where we're going, you're going to need different clothes."

Darcy was intrigued. "What does that mean?"

"That's for me to know and you to find out" was Bruce's mysterious reply.

Darcy laughed and shook her head. *He really was romantic,* she thought. And he looked especially great that day. His blond hair and brown eyes were set off by his dark skin, already tanned from skiing. And in jeans, a bright red sweater, and blue ski parka, he looked terrific.

"OK, give me a few minutes to change," she said. "I take it from your attire," she said, stressing the last word, "that I should dress for the out of doors?"

He grinned. "You take it correctly. Now hurry up."

Within minutes, Darcy had changed from the kilt and blouse to blue jeans and a turtleneck and sweater. She quickly pulled on the furry snow boots she had gotten for Christmas and ran back downstairs.

"How'd I do?" she asked breathlessly. She pulled on her ski jacket.

Bruce eyed her appreciatively. "Not bad. Not bad."

"Not bad?" Darcy waved a clenched fist in front of Bruce's face. "I'll give you 'not bad,' buster."

"OK. OK—terrific, I should say. How about some gloves?"

"Boxing gloves?" Darcy said as she pulled a pair of red mittens from her pocket.

He grinned. "Come on, let's go." He grabbed her hand, and they left the house.

As they stepped outside, Darcy caught her breath in the frigid air. But even more than the temperature, the scene itself was breathtaking. A fresh blanket of snow shrouded and softened the shapes around her house, and the expanse of white glistened in the blinding sunlight.

"Wow," she said breathily. "What a great day."

Bruce leaned over and kissed her ear. "This is only the beginning of a great day."

They climbed into Bruce's car, and Darcy glanced into the backseat as they started down the road. A picnic basket and blanket were on the floor.

"What's this?" she asked, starting to feel excited. She was dying to know what Bruce's surprise was.

"OK, I'll tell you. We're going to Hawaii."

Darcy laughed. She thought she had never been so happy. "Come on, McGinnis, out with it. Where are we going?"

"Would you believe to a funeral?"

Her mouth dropped open. "A fu— Oh, come on, Bruce, knock it off." Darcy twisted around in her seat so that she could get a choking hold on her boyfriend's neck. "If you don't tell me, I'll strangle you! Now *where are we going?*"

Bruce smiled at her calmly. "Right here."

Darcy raised her eyebrows and looked out the window. She hadn't paid any attention to their route while they'd been talking, but now she saw that they had arrived at the park entrance. Within minutes, they had pulled up at the base of Devil's Hill.

The snowy slope was covered with little kids, families, and high-school students in pairs.

Everyone was bundled up in scarves and colorful ski caps, and they were all sliding down the hill on anything and everything possible: toboggans, sleds, flying saucers, trays, and even sheets of plastic. With the sun beating down, it was a bright, cheerful scene in spite of the chilly air.

Her eyes widened. "We're going sledding!"

Bruce grinned. "Right you are, madam. Plus a picnic afterward to warm us up."

"Oh, Bruce!" She threw her arms around him. He knew how much she loved to sled, and he had planned their day around it. "You're something special."

He looked down into her eyes, his own eyes dancing with laughter. "I happen to think so, too."

"Oh, tell me about it, Mr. Modesty! Come on, let's get going!"

"Not until—"

Bruce leaned over as he opened the car door. Then spinning around quickly, he tossed a snowball over his shoulder at Darcy.

"Bruce, I'll kill you!" she shrieked.

She yanked open her door to escape, and within seconds, a spirited snowball fight was in progress. Bruce won by charging toward her through a barrage of snowballs and throwing her over his shoulder. He trotted with her to a snowbank and dropped her in it. Then he flopped down beside her, convulsed with laughter.

"OK, OK. *Uncle!*" she gasped breathlessly, pulling a strand of hair out of the corner of her mouth. Darcy smiled, squinting in the snow-reflected glare. *What a spectacular day,* she thought to herself. *I must be pretty lucky to have all this.* She hugged her arms around herself, and then jumped up, extending one mittened hand. "Let's sled, Fred."

Bruce got his old Flexible Flyer sled out of the trunk of the car where he had stashed it, and he and Darcy trudged up the hill and sledded down again and again, screaming with excitement as the snow sprayed out behind them. Bruce maneuvered the sturdy sled past the more cautious sliders and narrowly avoided plowing into a snowdrift on their last trip down.

As the sled came to a halt, Darcy and Bruce sat still for a moment, still treasuring the sensation of breathtaking flight. Then, leaning to the left, Darcy let herself fall over onto her side in the snow.

"Ohh . . . I've got snow up my wrists. Every part of me is warm except my wrists. That's always happened to me—ever since I was a little kid." She squinted up at Bruce. "I thought I was supposed to grow out of stuff like that."

"Maybe you haven't grown up yet. Maybe you're still just a little kid."

"Oh, yeah? I'll show you who's just a little kid!" With that, Darcy lunged forward and tackled Bruce off the sled, giving the finishing blow with a kiss on his cold cheek.

"A little kid, huh?" she asked, rolling over again onto the snow.

"Welllll . . ." Bruce sat up, a huge grin on his face. He cast his eye quickly over the people milling about on the hill and at the bottom. "Hey, there's Nancy. Nancy! Over here!"

As Darcy watched in disbelief, Bruce stood up and waved his arms over his head, gesturing for Nancy Piper to join them. She shook her head, as if wondering if this were a bad dream. "What is she doing here?"

Bruce sat down again on the sled. "Well, I told her we'd be here today and—"

"You *told* her?"

"Yeah, and I—"

"You *told* Nancy Piper what my surprise was going to be before I even knew about it?" Darcy's heart was pounding, and her face felt flushed.

A look of confusion crossed Bruce's features. "Well, sure, Darce. What's wrong with that?"

"Bruce, I'm com—"

"Hi, Bruce! Hi, Darcy! I bet you guys have been sledding for hours! Had your picnic yet?"

Nancy Piper stood before them, shielding her eyes from the blinding glare. Even squinting, Nancy managed to still have that Sniper look about her.

And Darcy, as hurt and angry as she felt, could see that Nancy's smile was triumphant—she had known Bruce's plans before Darcy had—and that smug grin made Darcy even more furious.

She jumped up. "Gee, Nancy. What a pity we have to leave. I see you came all alone, huh?"

Nancy's grin faltered for a moment. "Well I thought—"

"Too bad you'll have to sled by yourself. Bye." Darcy reached down to grab the sled's rope and started pulling it toward the parking lot.

As she trudged through the heavy drifts, her thoughts whirled around like windblown snowflakes. How could Bruce be so insensitive? How could he not see what an insult it was to have told Nancy their plans? And then to admit it? Why did he have to act like such a jerk sometimes?

She kicked angrily at a toppled snowman. *I bet Josh Foster would never do anything so tactless. He's a real gentleman, and he always seems to know just what to say—*

Darcy came to an abrupt halt. Josh? What made her start thinking about him? She looked around quickly. Bruce was just running to catch up with her.

"What's the big idea? Are you mad at Nancy for something? I swear, you always seem to get upset about the weirdest things." He was breathing heavily from plowing through the snow so quickly.

For a minute Darcy was too confused to speak. She still felt angry and hurt, but she was also sad for some reason. He never understood why she got mad, it seemed. Her shoulders sagged suddenly, and she felt very tired. She glanced up at Bruce from underneath her eyelashes. "I guess I'm just tired, that's all. Let's go home."

Chapter Four

"So, how much should we put away?"

Darcy leaned back and studied the sheet of figures in her hand. She shook her head, glancing up at Josh.

"How much do we have, anyway?" he asked, reaching for the paper.

"Well, fifteen thousand, altogether," Darcy answered slowly. "But we've got to cover everything with that."

Josh nodded. "Hmm. You're right. So . . ." He looked up, his forehead creased. "The apartment we can cover with our salaries, easy. Well, look, does it make sense to start with the bank account? I mean, we might not even have anything left to save once we're through."

"Oh, no. No way. We have to save money,

no matter what." Darcy sat up straighter in her chair and folded her arms across her chest. Her chin was lifted defiantly.

Her partner raised his eyebrows. "Sounds like you're pretty serious."

"Serious? Are you kidding? Look," she continued, her voice very earnest, "you know what kind of guy Webb is, right?"

"Well, actually I don't."

"You—" Darcy nodded. "Oh, yeah, I forgot. You're new. Well, he's certifiably wacko, OK? And he's liable to do anything. *Anything*," she stressed, shaking her head and smiling ruefully. "So we've got to be prepared. If he catches us with nothing in our savings account, he'll nail us."

Josh laughed. "OK, so we'll have to save something. But it might not be more than twenty-five cents. I hope you can handle that."

Darcy laughed, too. "I can handle it."

He shrugged. "OK. If you say so." He studied the sheet of figures again. "Well, I guess it comes down to what we want to do with it. Here, want some of this?" He held out a partially unwrapped block of what looked like nuts and grains stuck together.

"What is it?" Darcy asked cautiously, breaking off a piece and tasting it gingerly.

"It's called Wha Guru Choo, something my

mom's always eating." Josh's eyes twinkled. "Totally natural. Sesame seeds, honey—you name it, it's in there."

"Well, whatever it is, it's gluing my teeth together." Darcy tried using her hands to pry open her jaws, with only small success. "Ugh! Give me a break," she groaned, finally freeing her top teeth from her bottom teeth.

"Oh, yeah, I should've warned you about its adhesive effect."

The tone of Josh's voice made Darcy look up at him sharply. She chuckled. "You probably did this on purpose, so you wouldn't have to hear me talk. But it didn't work, see? I can still talk. Sort of."

One of Josh's rare smiles lit up his face. "I stand defeated. Or sit, I suppose," he corrected himself, patting the arms of his chair.

Darcy swallowed hard. "Ah, free at last. From now on, I'm sticking with mushy junk food that's filled with preservatives. That natural stuff could kill you." She carefully ran her tongue over her teeth.

"Nothing broken?"

With a wry grimace, she shook her head. "I wouldn't be surprised if you were trying to lock my jaws so I'd starve to death, and you'd inherit all the money. Or so you wouldn't have to go through with this dumb project."

"Don't be too sure."

Josh's face was turned away, and Darcy could not read his expression. But something in his voice had caught her ear. She shrugged. *It must be my imagination—as usual,* she decided. "Well, it's the kind of thing Bruce would do," she joked. "He can't stand this kind of stuff."

"Oh?"

She looked back at the page of calculations. *I guess it doesn't hurt to remind him once in a while,* she told herself silently. "Anyway, we still don't know what to do with the money—not that there really is any to speak of."

"Hey, that's my hard-earned savings you're talking about." Josh's voice shifted subtly again as he continued. "I work forty, maybe fifty hours a week down at the plant, an' I don't need to hear you beefing about that dough."

Darcy giggled and picked up his cue. "Aw, but, baby! We never have any fun no more. You never take me out to a nice place or nothing."

"Ah, gimme a break. Quit your belly-achin'."

"But, Josh, the kids don't have good sneakers! They say they gotta have leather hightops, and all I can afford to git 'em is grocery store canvas!"

"Ah, you know what you can do with the sneak—" Josh broke off, and the two collapsed into laughter, unable to keep up their act.

Across the room, a stern-faced librarian looked up from her work. With ferocious dignity, she raised one finger to her lips and shook her head at Darcy and Josh. She ostentatiously placed a Quiet Please sign in front of her on her desk.

"Ooops." Darcy giggled. She whispered hoarsely through her laughter. "Look what you did. Now she'll probably call the cops on us."

Josh held one hand tightly over his mouth until the last convulsive laugh died down. "Are you kidding? She *is* a cop. All right, all right." He sighed with a weak chuckle. "Let's get serious. No, really," he insisted, seeing Darcy still smirking as she tried to focus on the figures before her. "And no more of your loud-mouth yelling, either."

She relented. "OK. Let's be serious. I think we should really try to save five thousand dollars, no matter how much we have to scrimp on other stuff. I think it's important."

She looked down into Josh's face for signs

of agreement. He smiled faintly. "Whatever you say, boss."

"Good. So, five thousand dollars. We have to make some kind of financial goal."

"Now you're talking. We could invest it, like in stocks," Josh suggested.

But Darcy shook her head. "No way. On that much money the broker's fees would be too high a percentage."

Josh stared at her, openmouthed. "Oh? I didn't know I was speaking to an expert on the stock market."

She shrugged. "You're not. I'm just an expert at picking up phrases during TV commercials and repeating them." A mischievous smile curled her lips as she sorted through the bank flyers she had brought. "Why don't we just put it in a savings account—like a certificate of deposit, so we get higher interest. And we can't get at it until the time is up. You know, 'substantial penalty for early withdrawl.' "

"Yeah, they take you in front of a firing squad at dawn if you try to get at your dough."

Darcy gave a short chuckle. "Come on, I thought we were being serious."

"But I am!" Josh protested, holding out his

hands. "They really do that. I saw it on 'Sixty Minutes.' "

She glared at him silently for a moment. "All right, if you say so. As I was saying, then when the time is up, we can do something with the money."

A dreamy look came into Josh's eyes. "Like go to Madagascar."

"Huh?"

"OK, so maybe we don't go to Madagascar."

Darcy smiled serenely. "Maybe some of the smaller islands off the eastern coast of Africa, then."

Josh's eyes opened wide; he was obviously impressed. "I didn't think anyone even knew where Madagascar was."

"Ha! Are you kidding?" Darcy leaned forward eagerly. "I have a globe, and half the time I just look at it, trying to decide all the places I want to go."

"You want to travel, then, right?"

She closed her eyes. She could imagine herself in any setting: on camelback in the Sahara Desert, sailing a fishing boat in the Aegean Sea, dining in luxury on the famous Orient Express train, or viewing the ancient splendor of China from the Great Wall. Her fondest dream was to travel around the world, and Darcy Stevens was determined to make that dream come true someday.

Slowly she opened her eyes again and focused on Josh's face. She smiled. "Yeah, you could say that. I guess I want to travel more than anything else. I mean, who cares about possessions? You just have to take care of them." Smiling again, she shook her head. "I'd rather go to China than have a Ming vase."

He returned her grin. "Me, too. I always think about what I'd do if I won the lottery or something." He paused, as if he, too, were seeing himself in a far-off country. "And it's always travel."

Darcy cocked her head to one side. "Where would you go? Where's the first place you'd go if you won a million dollars?"

He laughed. "That's easy. Scotland, definitely." His brows drew together, as if he were trying to make up his mind. "Or Australia." He grinned sheepishly. "I'm not very good with languages."

"Well, I'm covered anywhere they speak French," Darcy said, leaning forward eagerly. "So don't worry about that. I'll interpret. France, Belgium—actually, lots of people speak French, anyway, so we could go tons of places."

Josh caught her gaze and held it. "I think you'd be great to travel with."

There was a brief pause as they looked intently at each other. For a moment Darcy couldn't think of anything to say. She wasn't sure if he was serious, or if he was just saying that to be polite. But either way, she didn't know how to respond.

"Darcy!"

She looked up, startled. Bruce was standing across the table from where they sat, an angry scowl on his face.

"Darcy, can I talk to you for a minute?"

Josh's face had become an impassive mask, and he merely shrugged when Darcy excused herself.

Darcy and Bruce walked across the hushed library to a small reading room. Bruce closed the door behind them and turned quickly to face Darcy.

"Just what was that all about?"

"What was what about? What are you talking about?" Darcy felt her face growing hot with anger.

"That—" Bruce gestured toward the closed door, and Darcy looked as if she could see Josh through it.

Bruce took a deep breath. "You two looked

pretty friendly a minute ago. Just what's going on between you, anyway?"

"What's going on—? Now wait a minute!" Darcy folded her arms and planted her feet more squarely on the floor. She stared into Bruce's face for a moment, as if trying to see what was going on in his mind. Then she shook her head slowly, trying to control her temper. "Bruce, I was talking to my partner about our social studies project. Which—as far as I can tell—is what you have also been doing on a pretty regular basis with *your* partner. And I haven't accused *you* of anything, have I?"

"No, because there's nothing to accuse me of!"

"What? Well, I think it stinks that you came barging in here like some jealous husband. Just who do you think you are, anyway?"

Bruce had taken a step backward, while Darcy let loose her barrage, and now he was blushing fiercely. "I just didn't like seeing you with him, that's all."

"Didn't like seeing me with him? Are you kidding me?" Darcy stared at him, her mouth open in disbelief. "What's all this possessive stuff anyway? Since when do you have to like—'seeing me'—with anybody?" She nearly tripped over her words in her haste to get them out. "I think that's pretty archaic, Bruce. Don't you? What is this, the Middle Ages?"

"OK, OK! You don't have to get so worked up about it, Darcy! Don't you think you're letting yourself get carried away?"

She closed her eyes. Somewhere in the back of her mind she heard her father joking about her terrible temper, but she ignored it. "Oh, terrific! Now I'm not just cheating on you, but I'm hysterical, too. Right? Well, maybe I'm not afraid to say what I feel! Maybe I'm not just a sweet little thing for you to play Mr. Neanderthal with. Maybe—" She broke off, suddenly unable to think of anything more to say.

She continued to stare at him, breathing heavily. He finally pulled a chair forward and sat down, his head between his hands. "I'm sorry, Darce. I'm sorry." He looked up, an expression of apology and pain on his face. "It's just that—"

The look of remorse in her boyfriend's eyes made Darcy's heart soften toward him again. It was really kind of sweet that he was jealous, she thought. *But, if only he trusted me a little more*. She sat down next to him, and he put his arm around her.

"I'm sorry, Darcy. I love you, that's all."

"Oh, I know. I understand," she mumbled

into his shoulder. She leaned back and looked into his face. Tenderly brushing a lock of hair from his forehead, she smiled. "Josh is just a friend, Bruce. We have to work together a lot, that's all. You know that."

"Yeah, I guess." He kissed her lightly on the nose.

"And, Bruce? I'm sorry, too—about—well, what I said. Sometimes I say dumb things when I get mad, that's all."

"It's OK, babe." He smiled. "Anyway, I was thinking about what you said. You know—about not seeing enough of each other. So I thought I'd stop by and see if I could drive you home."

"Hmm"—she rubbed her chin thoughtfully, as if trying to decide whether she should agree or not—"on one condition."

Bruce sat back and folded his arms across his chest. "OK, here it comes. What's the condition?"

"You have to take me to O'Henry's for a chocolate malted. With whipped cream," she added, trying to maintain a stern expression.

He reached for her hand. "Whatever you say, boss."

Darcy jerked back suddenly. *Boss.* That was exactly what Josh had called her a few minutes ago. *Am I really that bossy?* she wondered. She frowned. "Does everyone think I'm some kind of dictator?"

"Dictator?" Bruce brushed back the stray lock of blond hair from his eyes again. "No, it's just that when you get mad—look out!"

"You make me sound like some kind of mass murderer or something," Darcy pouted, only half-serious. She looked pleadingly at him. "I know I've got a bad temper," she admitted, "but I don't stay mad, you know."

"I know. That makes it even better," Bruce said, his voice husky. "We get to make up so often."

He pulled her toward him again and hugged her tightly. "Now, how about that malted?" he whispered into her hair.

Sighing, she brushed her hair back with her hands. "Sure. And, Bruce?"

"Yeah?"

"Let's really make an effort to spend more time together, even with this project hanging over our heads—OK?"

"Sure."

"I mean, we just seem to be getting in fights all the time, and I hate that."

Bruce sighed. "Me, too, Darce."

She bit her lip thoughtfully and looked around her, as if for the first time. Through the window she could see that the early twilight was falling fast. She stood up, then held her hand out to her boyfriend. "Let's go."

As they made their way across the library, Darcy glanced up into Bruce's face. His eyes were focused on Josh.

She quickly looked over to where her partner sat, seemingly engrossed in a book. For some reason, she had the impression that something was wrong—that he was mad at her—but she shrugged it off. *I told Josh at the beginning,* she reminded herself. *I have a boyfriend, and I'm going to be spending a lot of time with him. It's just too bad if I can't devote every waking moment to this project; he'll just have to get used to the idea.* She tightened her grip on Bruce's hand.

"Josh, I've got to go now," she said hurriedly, scooping up her books. "We'll talk tomorrow in class, OK?"

He glanced up briefly, his eyes flitting over Darcy and Bruce. "Sure," he said, looking down at his book again. "See you tomorrow. Catch you later, Bruce."

"Oh, uh—yeah." Bruce looked startled, and he quickly shrugged into his ski jacket. "Let's go, Darce," he said, taking her arm.

As they walked swiftly through the room, their arms linked, Bruce suddenly laughed. "That guy Josh is kind of weird, you know?"

Darcy stopped. She looked back. Josh's eyes seemed to have been following their progress across the room, but when he saw Darcy looking in his direction, he bent over his books again. "No, I don't know. Why do you say that?"

"I'm not sure. Forget it." He shrugged. "Let's not talk about Josh Foster anymore, OK?"

A heated reply rose to Darcy's lips, but she bit it back. *Oh, big deal,* she said to herself. *Just forget about him.*

Chapter Five

"I think Cliff Schoeller is the biggest jerk in the universe."

Darcy chuckled as she shut her locker. "Sandra, last week you were in love with Cliff Schoeller."

"Yeah, my mistake," Sandra replied with a sour grimace. "That was before I found out what a totally obnoxious person he is."

"You mean he doesn't like you anymore, right?"

Her friend gave her a murderous look as they started down the hallway, dodging with experienced finesse through the groups of students. "Listen, Darcy, just because you're hooked for life to one of the most popular guys in this school doesn't give you the right to be snotty with me." The lighthearted tone of Sandra's voice betrayed her words.

"Hmm." Darcy shrugged slightly and unconsciously shook her head. Hooked for life? Was she really hooked to Bruce for life? Everyone seemed to think they were a timeless couple, and she had always assumed so, too. "Darcy and Bruce 4-Ever." But the idea suddenly made her uncomfortable. It wasn't that she didn't love Bruce—of course she did. But sometimes she just wished . . .

Darcy shook her head again as if trying to shake off her unsettling thoughts. It was another moment before she realized Sandra had asked her a question. "What did you say?"

"I said what are you doing this afternoon?" Sandra repeated, giving her friend a quizzical look.

"Oh, I'm meeting Josh to go shopping—for Webb's class," she hurried to add, noticing Sandra's suspiciously raised eyebrows. "Purely a business meeting."

Sandra pushed open the outside door and snorted in disbelief. "Sounds more like 'extracurricular activities' to me."

"Sandra, will you stop? It's nothing like that!"

"If you say so."

There was an uncomfortable pause as the girls turned down the path to the parking lot. Stale, gray patches of snow lay forlornly by the wayside, and Darcy shivered inside her parka.

"You two are spending a lot of—"

"Sandra!" Darcy whirled to face her friend, her face burning. "Look—Josh and I are working on a big project, OK? Our whole semester grade depends on it. So it's really important for us to do a good job!"

For a moment the two girls glared at each other, the tension thick between them. Then Sandra shrugged, lowered her eyes, and started walking again.

"It's fine with me," she continued, casually looking off into the distance. "I only mention it because I think he seems like a pretty nice guy, that's all."

The tension broke, and Darcy burst out laughing. "You're too much, Grossman. You know that?"

A wide grin poked the dimple in Sandra's left cheek into view. "Yeah, I know. Hey, there's Josh—speaking of the devil," she added under her breath.

"I heard that," Darcy hissed, shooting her best friend a look of mock exasperation.

"I'll see you later, Darce." Just as they reached the spot where Josh Foster was waiting, Sandra headed off for a group of kids she had spotted ahead of them in the parking lot. But she looked back over her shoulder to give him a quick sizing up.

His eyes followed her retreating figure. "That's what I call good, old-fashioned Yankee hospitality," he drawled, giving Darcy a lopsided smile. "Something wrong with me today? Have I grown a tail since algebra?"

Standing next to Josh after her recent conversation—and her recent confusing thoughts—made Darcy feel slightly edgy. "Oh, Sandra's just like that—kind of abrupt. Don't pay any attention to her. Let's get out of here, OK?"

They headed in the direction of his car. He glanced at her once as they got into the car, but he didn't say anything. Darcy was grateful that he seemed to sense her unwillingness to talk. Some minutes later, after they had pulled out onto the highway, he broke the silence. "You'll have to tell me how to get there—I'm still not sure of my way around here sometimes."

"Oh, sure. No problem." Darcy spoke quickly, eager for any distraction. "Just take Exit Nine

A, and you'll see the mall as soon as you get off. It's 'the world's greatest indoor shopping experience' and all that. They really mean the *biggest*. You can't miss it."

"OK," he said again, his eyes on the road. They drove ahead in silence for a few minutes, gazing at the changing landscape. Then Josh spoke up quietly. "Is something bothering you, Darcy?" He looked over at her quickly before turning his attention to the traffic again. "I don't mean to pry, I just thought you might feel like talking."

Darcy leaned back against the door and studied him for a moment. *He really is a nice guy,* she thought. *He's—considerate. And sincere. And I can talk to him, too,* she decided. *He'll understand—he won't take it the wrong way.*

She laughed softly. "Well, it's pretty dumb, I guess. It's just that I seem to be getting a lot of grief lately about working with you so much. You know, from Bruce—and now Sandra." She stared out the window at the used-car lots and roadside restaurants they were passing. "I mean, here we are just working on a social studies project, and everyone assumes we're running off to elope or something." She turned her head to look at him. "Dumb, isn't it? People can be so suspicious."

"Yeah, that sure is dumb."

There was another long pause. Darcy suddenly wondered if she should have just not said anything. *Me and my big mouth*, she scolded herself. *I wonder if I hurt his feelings. But, gosh, it's not my fault if the guy likes me*, she told herself crossly. She peered at Josh intently. Was she right in thinking that he liked her?

"Oh, look, here's the exit," she announced with some relief.

In a few minutes they were standing within the muffled uproar of a big department store, and they began to talk about why they had come to the mall.

Darcy pulled her notebook out of her shoulder bag and pointed at the first item on the list. "One one-bedroom apartment, here we go." She was grateful that they had a specific goal now.

Josh surveyed the lush displays of merchandise spread out all around them. "Are you sure we can afford this stuff with only five thousand dollars?"

"Of course. That's what we decided, remember?" She smiled, realizing that she sounded a lot more confident than she actually felt. "At least we can try," she added softly, after a moment's deliberation. She looked around her, then pulled her bag up higher on her arm in a firm, businesslike manner. "Come on, this shouldn't be too hard. Five thousand dollars is a lot of money."

"You know, in real life, we'd get to raid our parents' attics for most of this stuff," Josh complained good-naturedly. "If you ask me, it's unfair that Mr. Webb is making us start from scratch."

As Darcy laughed, she was aware of a pulsing beat suddenly filling the air. They both turned. "Hey, let's check out the electronics department," she urged, leading the way.

"Whoa, look at this," Josh said a moment later. He had stopped in front of a gleaming black-and-chrome tower of stereo equipment, which was studded with winking green and red lights. "This," he said, nodding in obvious appreciation, "is an awesome system. And look, Darcy, it's on sale," he added, giving his "wife" a hopeful glance.

"Hmm. You're right. Eight hundred and ninety-nine dollars seems like a really fair price for such a good stereo. It's got everything —state of the art." Darcy ran her finger across a row of shiny buttons and smiled at her partner. "I think we should get it. I mean, after all—we really need one, and this is such a good deal. It makes sense," she concluded, nodding her head. "Why settle for some piece of junk we'd just have to replace in a couple of years, right?"

Josh agreed eagerly. "Absolutely. OK, write that down—eight hundred ninety-nine dollars. What do you think the tax is?"

"Oh, come on! Do we have to worry about that?"

"All right." Josh ran a hand through his thick brown hair. "Let's call it nine hundred dollars."

Darcy grinned. "Good idea." She opened the notebook, jotted down the price, then glanced up to look around again. "Oh, look! Come here." In her excitement, she grabbed Josh's hand and dragged him across the electronics department to a wall full of microwave ovens. "These are so great. We have one at home. What do you say?"

"I don't know, Darcy," Josh said in a hesitant voice. Then he shrugged. "Oh, OK. Why not."

"You won't be sorry, honest. It'll be great." Darcy smiled at the tall, lanky boy in front of her. He returned her smile, his intense, blue-brown eyes gazing into hers. Suddenly, she realized they were still holding hands, and she released hers gently. "Let me just write this down. Now, four hundred eighty-five dollars," she said, checking the tag on the oven she wanted. "I know it's kind of extravagant, but they save you so much time when you're cooking." She glanced up swiftly but Josh wasn't looking at her anymore.

"It's fine with me, really," he said, turning back. "Now, what do you say we get some practical stuff," he suggested with a grin.

"Oh, absolutely." Darcy nodded. "From now on, we have to concentrate on strictly practical things. Although," she added thoughtfully, "the microwave really does make sense."

"Well, so does the stereo!"

"Can I help you kids with something?"

A small, bald salesman in a brown suit had approached them silently, and Darcy and Josh were startled to find him suddenly standing before them. He wiped his palms with a handkerchief he had drawn from his pocket and eyed them nervously.

"Oh, uh—"

"We're just shopping for our new apartment," Josh cut in before Darcy could explain. He put one arm around her shoulders in a possessive hug and gave her a squeeze. "We just got married."

The salesman looked quickly from Josh to Darcy and back to Josh again. He had a skeptical expression on his face. Clearing his throat, he said, "Oh. I see. Yes, how very nice."

Darcy could feel an uncontrollable giggle start to rise in her throat, and she nudged Josh lightly in the ribs with her elbow.

"That's right, sweetheart," he said, ignoring the jab and grinning down at her. "My wife would like to buy this microwave oven," he continued, addressing the salesman. "Could you tell us something about its features?"

The man ran a hand over his bald head and smiled feebly. "Oh, I see. How very nice. Well, this model has an automatic defrost setting, a temperature probe, and this carousel inside here"—he paused and blinked rapidly—"it's very hi-tech."

Josh beamed at him, and in a perfect imitation of the salesman's reedy voice, replied, "I see. How very nice."

The giggle suddenly erupted from Darcy's lips, and she coughed loudly, trying to disguise it. "Honey, I think I've changed my mind," she gasped, twisting out from under Josh's arm. "Could we have a minute to talk about it, please?" she asked the salesman, trying very hard to control her voice.

"Oh. Yes, of course. I'll be just over here."

Darcy and Josh watched as the salesman shuffled away. He glanced suspiciously over his shoulder at them a couple of times, then smiled hesitantly and gave a little wave as he positioned himself behind a glass display counter.

"Josh Foster, I will kill you for this!" Darcy hissed between clenched teeth. She was afraid she wouldn't be able to keep her laughter in check any longer. "Let's get out of here."

He grinned impishly at her. "Well, I'll just tell the gentleman we're no longer interes—"

"No! Let's just go!"

She grabbed his arm and marched him out of the department. Josh turned once to wave at the puzzled salesman before they rounded a corner and passed out of sight into the furniture department.

Once safely out of view, the two collapsed onto an overstuffed, light-green sofa and laughed until tears streamed down their cheeks. Passing shoppers cast quizzical looks in their direction, but that only seemed to make them laugh harder.

"I thought southerners were supposed to be polite," Darcy giggled.

Josh put up a weak protest. "But I was. I

was perfectly polite to him. Didn't you see me wave goodbye?"

"Oh, yeah—right." Remembering the bland little man, Darcy lapsed into hysterics again. "OK, OK. Let's get serious now," she finally managed to say. As she wiped a tear from the corner of her eye, a chuckle threatened to resurface, but she managed to squelch it. "Now," she announced firmly, opening her notebook on her knees, "now we've got to start being practical about this. Are you going to be serious?"

Josh pulled himself up as straight as he could on the soft-cushioned sofa. He took a deep breath. "OK. Right." He swallowed hard, then grinned at Darcy. "OK, now I'm being totally serious. What about this sofa?"

"Josh, come on!"

He tried to look hurt. "No, really! It's nice, don't you think?"

For the first time, Darcy actually looked at the sofa on which they had taken refuge. The light green of the calico upholstery was one of her favorite colors, and she said as much to Josh.

"It also makes a great backdrop for your hair, you know," he said, reaching out to tug at a lock of it.

"Cut that out, mister." She batted his hand away, reaching for the price tag. "It really is comfortable. You're right. But Josh—!" Looking back at him with a stricken expression, she dropped the tag. "It's twelve hundred dollars!"

"So what? We've got that much." He wiped the grin from his face "No, I mean it. We need a sofa, right?"

Darcy shrugged, still unconvinced. But as she leaned back into the dreamy softness, she nodded.

"Good. So we'll get this one." He reached for her notebook and marked down the item and the price. "I think we're doing a pretty good job so far, don't you?"

For the next twenty minutes, they roamed the furniture, carpet, and china departments, jotting down items that caught their eye. Then they returned to their sofa and sat down to total up their purchases. "Let's just see how much we've got left," Darcy said, biting the end of her pen.

After a few minutes they looked up at each other in alarm.

"Five thousand twenty-five dollars! Josh, what are we going to do?" Darcy wailed, dropping her list of purchases in disgust. "We're already over budget, and we don't have nearly enough stuff yet!"

"Hmm." Taking the list, Josh looked it over again and shook his head. "We'll can the oriental rug, first of all."

"But it's a gorgeous rug!"

"Yeah, and it's also six hundred and twenty-five bucks."

Darcy reached for the list again. "All right. All right. The stereo is out, then, too—Josh, would you look at the stuff we bought: a stereo, a microwave oven, a sofa, an oriental rug, a water bed, and four place settings of china." She chuckled softly. "Boy, did we blow it!"

"Well, at least we tried, huh?" Josh said, holding his hands in front of his face, appealing for mercy.

Darcy slapped her palm to her forehead, as she surveyed their list one more time. "Ugh. How could we be so dumb? It's a good thing we didn't really buy any of this junk," she added, "because we'd end up returning absolutely everything. We didn't even get any pots and pans. No chairs. No tables. No lamps. No sheets or towels. No vacuum cleaner. No—"

"Enough!" Josh buried his head in his arms. "This is depressing," he mumbled, his head still down. "Do we have to start all over again?"

Darcy smiled ruefully and nodded her head. "All over again. But this time, let's make a new list first. And then we'll only buy the cheapest stuff we can get."

"I thought newlyweds were supposed to 'live on love.' " Josh turned his head to one side and grinned up at her. "Haven't you heard that?"

He received a stern look for an answer. But Darcy added, "Don't forget this was an arranged marriage, Josh. Now let's get moving."

When they had finished picking out a set of aluminum pots and pans, plastic dinnerware, a box spring and mattress, dining table and folding chairs, they had fairly well covered the essentials. But they were both disappointed to find just how close to the bone they had had to cut. There were no luxuries on their new list—no stereo, no microwave, no oriental rug, no water bed—and nothing expensive.

"This is pretty pathetic," Josh complained.

"Yeah, but we furnished the whole apartment within our budget. Don't you think that's kind of amazing?"

Darcy's partner grinned and shook his head. "Amazing, Darcy. Truly amazing."

She laughed and held out her hand for him to shake. "Good teamwork."

They turned toward the exit, filled with the satisfaction of success. Darcy stole a look in Josh's direction. "And you know what the best part of it is?"

"What?"

"This'll blow Bruce and the Sniper right out of the water!"

Josh shouted with laughter as they passed through the door of the department store.

Chapter Six

Several weeks later, Darcy looked out the classroom window and was surprised to notice a purple-and-white sprinkling of crocuses showing under the birch trees. And now that she thought about it, she remembered that it seemed almost warm when she had walked to the art building that morning. *The semester's going pretty fast,* she thought. *I can't believe it's almost spring.*

A ripple of laughter pulled her attention away from the window. Mr. Webb had obviously delivered another one of his famous one-liners; she could see Bruce still smiling. As she looked at the profile of the face that had become so familiar to her, she felt a little tug at her heart. Something was wrong, and they both knew it. This project, with all of its research and note-taking, was just taking up too much of their time.

Remembering what had happened the night before, Darcy sighed. Bruce had come over to watch TV with her, and they had curled up, nestled close to each other, on the couch in the den. Everything should have been perfect: there was a romantic movie on, the lights were low, and they had the house to themselves. But they had hardly spoken a word all evening. Oh, they'd both tried talking about how delicious dinner had been or how great it was that the weather was starting to get so warm, but all their conversation had seemed to fall flat.

She tapped one finger softly on her desk. *It's this project.* Darcy sighed again, thinking to herself. *If I'm not filling up three-by-five note cards or doing research at department stores, I'm thinking about it twenty-four hours a day. It's so hard to find time for Bruce.*

"When you're finished," Mr. Webb was saying. "So, without further ado, the first quiz—"

Darcy sat bolt upright in her seat. Quiz? Had she really heard Mr. Webb say the word *quiz*? She felt her face flush as she looked quickly around. "What did he say?" she whispered hoarsely to Josh.

He leaned across the aisle. "Don't worry, it's really just a status report." With a reassuring smile, Josh sat up straight again and looked at Mr. Webb.

Darcy took a deep breath and scolded herself for daydreaming in her most important class. With a firm resolution to pay strict attention until the last second of the period, she focused on what Mr. Webb was saying.

"Now, I suppose you've come to expect slightly erratic behavior from me," he was saying, holding up one hand for silence and smiling broadly.

There was a chorus of laughing protest from the class before he could continue. "And I guess some of you think you've been pretty clever about becoming invisible whenever I ask questions. However"—his hand went up again, and he pointed to the class, sweeping his arm slowly to take in every student in turn—"the laws of probability say the odds are running out on some of you. So!" He spun around and pointed straight at one couple. "Peter and Amanda! Report!"

Heads turned to that side of the classroom, and a few scattered giggles made the faces of the two of them turn even redder than they already were. Amanda, a short, dark-haired girl, cleared her throat and pulled nervously at a gold chain she wore around her neck. "Well, I mean, what do you want to know, Mr. Webb."

The teacher smiled. "Oh, everything."

There were a few more giggles, and Peter and Amanda squirmed visibly in their chairs. "Well, you see, it's like—" Peter began, absently opening and closing a textbook.

"Yes? It's like what?" Mr. Webb probed mercilessly.

Darcy looked over at Josh. He met her gaze, and they exchanged a look that said, *Thank heavens, it's not us!*

Peter shook his head and sank into complete, crimson-faced silence.

Mr. Webb leaned back against his desk and folded his arms. "Well, let's see if I can help you along here. Do you have some place to live?"

"Well, she—"

"Mr. Webb, Peter—"

"Whoa! One at a time, please. I gather there's a little trouble in paradise," Mr. Webb said behind his hand to the rest of the class. He grinned broadly before he focused on his victims again. "Amanda, let's hear it from you."

Amanda shot her partner a venomous look, then she addressed Mr. Webb. "Well, we tried to. I wanted to live with my parents—to save money—but he said we couldn't. He wanted to live in a cabin in the woods!"

There was an outburst of laughter that brought the color out even darker on Peter's face.

"Good, OK, fine." Mr. Webb cut off Amanda's protest with a smile and turned to the other students. "Let's have a show of hands here. Does everyone have *some* place to live?"

All hands went up. Josh gave Darcy the thumbs-up sign.

"Let's see. OK, does everyone have a savings account? No matter how much is in it?"

Only about half the couples did. Darcy raised her eyebrows and smiled at Josh as she put up her hand. She could take the credit for that one.

Mr. Webb shook his head sadly, but the sympathy in his voice did not reach his intense, laughing eyes. "Tsk, tsk. You young people today are so improvident. All right, every couple who does not have a savings account, hear this—the husband has been laid off, and you will have to live on the wife's earnings."

A chorus of groans rang out. One girl complained to her husband, "I told you again and again. But, no! You wouldn't do it! Now, look!"

"Well, that's a relief, anyway," Josh whispered across the aisle. "We couldn't have kept making car payments on just your salary."

Darcy laughed shortly. "I'll say. Our whole budget depends on both of us working."

He nodded, and Darcy looked down at her notes. That budget had taken so much time, she remembered with a smile. They'd covered everything. Everything! She shook her head as she recalled the afternoons spent going back and forth over the details. What about taking out a loan? What about paying for utilities? What about charitable donations? Darcy had laughed at that one, suggesting that they ought to be receiving them instead of giving them. But Josh had said it was important to him. So it had gone into the budget.

And she remembered the extra effort Josh had made, talking to bank and store managers and used-car salesmen, asking questions and looking for advice. His reserves of patience and politeness seemed bottomless. She could almost hear him saying in that lilting southern way of his: *Thank y'all so much for your help and your understanding. I'm very much obliged.*

She leaned over toward Josh again. "Are you sure we thought of everything?"

"Relax, Darcy. I'm positive."

"Well, I wish I could be as optimistic as you," she whispered with a wry grin.

"Now," Mr. Webb was saying as he turned from the blackboard. "Have you ever noticed how you can have everything planned just perfectly, and then along comes life and throws you a curve ball?" He was wearing one of his deceptively sweet-and-innocent smiles—the kind of smile that said to his class—Look out!

Fighting a creeping sense of panic, Darcy tried to compose her face. *What exactly is he driving at this time? We have everything planned perfectly.*

"Yes, indeed," he continued, still smiling satanically. "It never fails to intrigue me how some people think they've got *life* under control." He opened a drawer in his desk and pulled out a shoe box as he went on. "This box contains thirteen slips of paper. Seven of them are blank. Six have an *X* written on them. Would the 'wives' please line up here to draw from the box?"

Darcy shot Josh a nervous look as she

pushed her chair back. Tugging anxiously at her denim skirt, she paused beside his chair. "Which do you think is better, blank or *X*?" she asked, swallowing hard.

He shrugged, biting his lower lip. "Beats me. Just make sure you get the right one, or you're out in the cold," he said, looking up at her with a grin.

"Yeah, right." Darcy joined the line of girls inching forward. When it was her turn to choose, she glanced up at Mr. Webb. "I think you enjoy watching people suffer."

Her teacher threw his head back and laughed. "I think you're right, Darcy. Why else would I be in this line of work?"

With an airy smile, Darcy retorted, "Maybe you're just a little bit sadistic."

He bowed. "That, of course, is a definite possibility. Please help yourself to a slip."

Hoping her smile disguised her feeling of dread, Darcy slowly unfolded the small square. She turned it over and over, as if unable to believe the paper was blank on both sides. As she reached her seat, she handed the slip to Josh with a small shrug. "Looks like we're in the clear, whatever that means."

"Now, about those pieces of paper. Will those couples who drew a blank please stand up."

Darcy drew a deep breath as she pushed

her chair back yet again. Josh stood next to her, and soon seven couples were standing, looking more than a little anxiously at the teacher.

He beamed at them. "Congratulations. You're going to have a baby."

A shock wave of panic ran through the seven standing couples, and seconds later, an aftershock of laughter and relief rippled among the childless ones.

"Mr. Webb, I just lost my job. Now I'm having a *kid*?" wailed a boy in the back row who had already been singled out for not opening a savings account.

"But I wouldn't—" wailed his partner.

"You're kidding!" said another girl, who was still staring at the blank sheet of paper in her hand.

"What are we going to do?" gasped a boy sitting behind Josh.

"Oh, no." Darcy sat down again slowly, shaking her head in disbelief. Their whole budget—carefully, precisely worked out over the past weeks, provided for two people—not two people and a baby.

She dropped her head down on her arms. "Josh! I can't believe it!"

"Me, either. Somehow, I just don't think of you as a mommy."

"Mommy!" Her head came up, and she stared openmouthed at her partner, as the clamor went on around them. But she could see the smile in his amazing blue-and-brown eyes. "You're a fine one to talk, Daddy," she said, chuckling. But the laugh soon turned into a moan. "I can't believe it. We'll have to redo the whole thing!"

"All right, folks. Let's settle down, now." An impish grin had spread over Mr. Webb's face, and he hopped up on the edge of his desk to survey the class. "I'm sorry about my guerrilla tactics," he said, his voice sounding far from apologetic. "But it's important for you not to get too sure of yourselves. I know it's great to be prepared and think you've covered all the bases. I do want you to do that. But if, somehow, I've led you to think you can have complete control over your lives, then I've given you a bum steer. I'm afraid it just isn't possible to plan for every one of life's little quirks. None of us lives in a vacuum, after all; there are forces beyond our control all around us. And sometimes they explode right in the middle of our neatly ordered existences." He illustrated his point with a surprisingly realistic explosion sound effect, which relieved some of the tension in the room.

He patted the desk top and pushed himself off onto the floor. "So, you'll have to figure out what kind of an impact this is going to have on you now."

"Mr. Webb," asked one of the now-expectant "wives," "does this mean we—the girls—have to stop working?"

He paused for a moment. "Well, no. I don't suppose so—unless you want to. What I mean is, well, medically speaking, there's no reason why you can't work pretty much up until the delivery date."

Darcy shook her head. This was crazy! They all talked as if this were really happening! But she had to admit that when she and Josh had been spending all those hours doing their research and preparing their report, they had been as serious as if it really had been their hard-earned money they had been budgeting, their own future they had been planning, real decisions they had been making. And every time they'd talked about their "vacation"—when they were going to take some fabulous trip somewhere—she'd always felt that it was really going to happen.

"But afterward, of course," he continued, "you'll be at home with the baby for a while."

Darcy's hand shot up, and she voiced a

question that had just occurred to her. "What about maternity leave and compensation and child care at the office—stuff like that? Do we get any of those things?"

She heard Josh chuckle softly next to her. "Go for it, Darcy," he whispered.

"Well, Darcy, that's a good question. There's quite a national debate about it, too, in fact. Do you think you should still receive your salary if you aren't working?"

"Well, I don't—" She looked at Mr. Webb, trying to figure out what she thought was fair.

He moved around behind his desk and sat down in his chair. "Let me ask you this. If employers were required to grant maternity leave to all female employees, pay their salaries, find temporary replacements, and guarantee that they would have their jobs back— well, how do you think that would effect a decision on whether to hire a man or an equally qualified woman?"

Darcy shook her head. "It doesn't seem fair, Mr. Webb."

Smiling gently, the teacher nodded. "You're right. But to solve this problem for now," he continued in a lighter tone, "you'll all be on summer vacation when the time comes and out of this class. So don't worry about it. Yes, you get to keep your salaries. And," he finished as the bell rang, "that's all for now, folks."

"You're turning into a feminist, Darcy."

"Yeah, right." Darcy leaned back in her big wooden chair, surveying the now-familiar view from their table in the library. She looked at him questioningly. "You act as if that's something you approve of."

Josh folded his arms over his chest and pretended to look offended. "You know, Darcy, not everyone from the South still thinks he lives on a plantation. Some of us have actually moved into the twentieth century."

She laughed. "Oh, shut up. Now, what are we going to do about this stupid baby, anyway?"

"I'm overwhelmed by your maternal instincts," Josh said, teasing her with a sarcastic smile. But he was suddenly serious. "This is a lot of work, you know. Somehow babies manage to take over completely, no matter what you do, so we're going to have to be even more careful than we were before. We'll have to budget for a crib, and baby clothes, and baby food—stuff like that."

The seriousness of Josh's tone intrigued

Darcy. Leaning forward, she asked, "Just what makes you such an expert on babies, anyway?"

He looked off across the room for a brief moment, fiddling with the pencil in his hand. "Well, I have a little brother. He's three now."

Darcy gasped. "You're kidding! I didn't know that—you never told me!"

Meeting her gaze steadily, Josh replied. "Well, you never asked, I guess."

Darcy ignored the feeling she had that she should have known by now what his family was like. "Well, I want to meet him," she decided. "I love little kids. What's his name?"

He chuckled. "You're going to love this—it's Beau, short for Beauregard."

"Oh, you're kidding," Darcy groaned. "Sounds like something right out of *Gone With the Wind*. So, do I get to meet him?"

"Maybe you will sometime, who knows? Anyway, let's get back to this you-know-what budget."

As Josh began compiling a list of baby necessities, his face took on the look of intense absorption Darcy had come to know. And now there was a new element. There was a tenderness in his voice that, she suddenly realized, spoke of his love for his little brother Beau. Darcy studied his face as he spoke, hardly hearing him, and thought about the hours and hours she had spent with him.

He turned suddenly and found her staring at him. Their eyes locked for one long moment, before Darcy broke contact, blushing to the roots of her hair.

"Darcy, I—"

"Oh, no! Look what time it is!" she gasped, groping frantically for her books. "I'm supposed to meet Bruce in twenty minutes." She turned and fled blindly from the library.

Chapter Seven

"Well, Bruce, we've missed seeing you on Thursday nights lately." Mr. Stevens unfolded his napkin and smiled at Bruce and Darcy.

"Yeah, well, you know about our projects for social studies, and it's been keeping us both pretty busy."

"Here, Bruce, have some salad."

"Thanks, Mrs. Stevens," Bruce replied, taking the big wooden bowl that she passed to him.

Darcy watched him from across the table. Their Thursday night dinners had been a tradition for a long time; she knew her parents felt that Bruce was almost part of the family. They had told her so often enough.

"You know, I was telling Darcy the other day how funny it seemed not having you around so much," her father continued, apparently oblivious of the uneasiness he had just created.

Darcy and Bruce exchanged an uncomfortable smile across the table. *It's just a matter of time*, Darcy told herself firmly. *When this semester is over, we'll be back to normal. I know it.*

"So what exactly is this marriage project about, anyway? Sounds pretty ridiculous to me." Mr. Stevens placed his knife and fork squarely on his plate and looked inquiringly from Darcy to Bruce and back again. "And how come Webb didn't let you two be partners? That would seem reasonable to me."

"Well, you see, Mr. Stevens—"

"Mr. Webb did it randomly, Dad," Darcy cut in impatiently. "He didn't want us to work with anybody we knew."

Her father picked up his knife and fork again. "So what's your partner like, anyway. What's his name again?"

"Josh Foster, dear," put in Mrs. Stevens from the end of the table. She smiled sympathetically at her daughter.

Darcy shrugged. "He's OK." She looked stonily down at her plate.

"So, fill me in. I'm curious to know just

how they run a social studies class with this kind of gimmick."

"Dad, come on! I've been spending practically every waking hour on this stuff. For once, let's just not talk about it, OK?"

Her father sat back, looking surprised, and ran one hand through his russet-red hair. "What's wrong?"

"I just don't want to talk about it. OK?" Darcy turned pleading eyes to her mother, silently asking for help in changing the subject.

"Bruce, how about some more mashed potatoes, hmm?" Deftly, Mrs. Stevens swept a serving dish in front of Bruce and spoke to her husband at the same time. "The oil man came today, and he suggested having some work done to the furnace."

"Oh, did he? Well—"

As her parents got into a heated discussion about the furnace and the radiators, Darcy let her mind wander. Toying with her pot roast and beans, she watched Bruce devour his second helping of mashed potatoes and gravy. She barely heard the voices around her, as she pondered the face of the boy she had known for so long.

He's so cute, she thought. *He's so adorable. I just wish he had a better sense of humor. I just wish he were more like Josh.*

Josh is always so funny, he just picks up on things and goes with them. Sometimes I feel as though I have to explain every joke to Bruce. Maybe Josh isn't quite as good-looking, but I almost wonder whether that matters at all. He seems to be able to read my mind sometimes. And he always knows just what to say.

Bruce looked up and caught her eye. As their gaze held, a tender smile crossed Bruce's face. But Darcy felt her heart pounding. *I love Bruce,* she told herself stubbornly. *I love Bruce.*

She looked away suddenly, unable to meet Bruce's eyes any longer. *But if I love Bruce,* she continued silently, *why, why don't I have the same feelings that I used to have?*

"How about you, Darcy? Have you got any good baby-sitting jobs lined up for summer vacation?"

Darcy jumped slightly, caught off guard by her father's question. She felt her face redden. "Dad, it's still a couple of months away. I haven't really thought about it yet." *But now that you mention it,* she added to herself, *I think I'll spend the summer putting this relationship back together. All it needs is a good dose of some time together. Then we'll fall in love with each other all over again, and everything will be back to normal.*

She sighed. "I guess I'll be lining something up pretty soon."

"Well, why don't you think about it while you and Bruce are doing the dishes, OK?" Mrs. Stevens suggested with a smile. "You do remember how, don't you?" she added as Darcy remained rooted to her chair, lost in thought.

"Oh, yeah. Sure, Mom."

As Darcy and Bruce got up to clear the table, Mrs. Stevens shot her daughter an inquiring look. But Darcy just smiled and hurried into the kitchen.

The dishwasher was running loudly enough to make it difficult to talk, and Darcy went through the motions of scouring the pots and pans in the sink with a steady, mechanical intensity. And she didn't stop until the last pot was scrubbed to a mirror finish. Only then did she look at Bruce, who was drying the pots as she was handing them to him.

He glanced at her, a worried frown creasing his forehead. "Are you mad at me about something?"

"'No."

"Well, then, what's wrong?" he asked, folding the dish towel. "You've been acting kind of funny all night."

"What's that supposed to mean?" she snapped instantly regretting her tone.

As he hung the towel on the rack, Bruce stared at her, perplexed.

With a heavy sigh, Darcy shook her head and stepped forward to wrap her arms around him. "I'm sorry, Bruce. I must just be depressed. I feel as though we never see each other anymore, and we never seem to be able to talk."

"Oh, Darcy. It's this stupid social studies project. You know that." But the tone of his voice was not as convincing as Darcy had hoped it would be. It was almost as if he was trying to convince both of them that their only problem was the project. "Come on, let's go watch TV."

Relieved that they wouldn't have to talk anymore, Darcy agreed. They sat in front of the television and stared at the screen with unusual concentration, as if their lives depended on taking in every bit of the nature program they were watching. But their silence had an edge of uneasiness. There was something unsaid between them, and neither of them quite knew what it was or how to talk about it.

At nine o'clock Bruce left for home. And as he gave her a quick kiss at the door, Darcy found herself almost glad that he had left early. "What a relief," she muttered as she closed the door.

But immediately she realized what she had said and stood in the front hall shaking her head, horrified. For a moment, she found herself unable to think or move. "What is wrong with me?" she moaned. But she finally decided she was just tired. Heaving a deep sigh, she wandered back into the den.

"Anything good on?" her mother asked, coming in to join her.

"Hmm," Darcy stared at the set, scarcely aware of her mother's presence.

"Darcy, are you all right?"

"Hmm."

"Darcy, look at me, please."

A note of concern gave Mrs. Stevens's voice a hard edge, and Darcy looked up obediently, roused from her somber mood.

An excuse had already formed itself on Darcy's lips. But she suddenly felt she had to talk, really talk, to someone. Darcy rose from her chair and curled up next to her mother on the sofa, resting her head on her mother's shoulder.

From that safe warmth, Darcy surveyed the

room she had spent so much of her life in. The botanical prints on the walls, the over-stuffed paisley-print easy chairs, and the cheerful little fluted lampshades all whispered "security and love" to Darcy. She drew a deep breath.

"Remember when I was little and something on TV scared me? I'd come and sit really close to you, and you'd tell me everything was OK."

Mrs. Stevens put one arm around her daughter and stroked her hair. "Is something scaring you now?"

A short, painful laugh was Darcy's answer. "Well, not exactly scaring me. *Confusing,* I guess, is more like it." She looked down at her mother's slender, graceful hands, the hands that had soothed her for almost seventeen years. She looked up, searching the loving face turned toward hers.

"Want to tell me about it? Maybe I can help unconfuse you."

Darcy shook her head. She wasn't sure anyone could do that. "Well—when you love someone, do you feel love all the time? I mean, are you always in love?"

Mrs. Stevens let her breath out slowly. "Whew. The sixty-four-thousand-dollar question, huh?"

Darcy was silent. She was hoping against hope that her mother could somehow make everything better. Mrs. Stevens sighed and leaned her head back against the cushions.

"Well, honey, I think—yes, I think that magical, incredible feeling you have when you first fall in love does fade a little bit although it should resurface every now and then—as sort of a reminder," she added with a tender, reminiscent smile. "But that level of emotion is pretty hard to sustain forever. It's bound to mellow somewhat. But, yes, I think you should feel some of that love all the time. And if you don't, then maybe you should ask yourself how you really feel about that person."

Darcy nodded, biting her lip. "But . . ." She trailed off, not knowing how to express her confusing and bewildering thoughts.

Her mother lifted her chin with one gentle hand and looked into Darcy's eyes. "Sweetheart, it is possible to fall out of love, you know," she said quietly.

A painful thudding in her heart made Darcy wince. "Mom, that's not it, really. Really," she insisted, fighting tears.

Shaking her head, Mrs. Stevens sighed. She kissed Darcy's forehead. "Darcy, honey, just try to listen to your heart."

Then the tears came. Sobbing, Darcy ran

from the den and stumbled upstairs. "I love you, Bruce. I love you," she repeated between her sobs. "I do."

The weather became warmer and warmer as the semester drew rapidly to a close. Looking back on it later, Darcy would remember spring as a rushing whirl of faces: Mr. Webb, grinning and gesticulating in front of the class; Bruce, wearing a frown instead of a smile most of the time; and Josh Foster, chewing thoughtfully on the end of a pencil and smiling whenever they solved some irritating problem, like how to pay the grocery bill and still have enough left over for a layette.

Josh and Darcy had now finished taking notes, organized the three-by-five index cards, and made a rough draft of their written report. But there was a renewed rush of intensity as the finishing touches were added. And Darcy and Bruce were spending even less time together.

Meanwhile, the dogwoods and daffodils bloomed outside. On the way home from school, Darcy noticed little kids wearing their coats on their heads like capes, reveling in the warmth of the sunshine on their bare arms. She had put away her own winter wardrobe and was wearing cotton skirts with short-sleeved shirts, and the school hallways echoed with a constant, expectant buzz.

But in spite of the thrill of spring fever, Darcy found herself torn in two directions. More and more, it seemed, being with Bruce was becoming burdensome. They didn't seem to be able to talk to each other easily, and their dates felt like obligations. When they kissed good night, Darcy felt a faint feeling of regret. A growing suspicion had begun to nag at her: Maybe it wasn't going to work, after all.

On the other hand, it was the hours of intense work with Josh that Darcy looked forward to. As they neared the final presentation, they became even more wrapped up in their mock marriage. They spent hours polishing up their twenty-page report and verifying last-minute details on the phone. Frequently Josh stopped her in the hall between classes to tell her of a new element they could use. They always had a smile for each other, and Darcy had begun to feel that the project was the most important thing in her life.

But every time that thought occurred to her, Darcy immediately contradicted herself. *My relationship with Bruce is more important,* she insisted. *Much more. This is just a temporary project. When the semester is over,*

Josh and I will go our separate ways. This is nothing more than a homework assignment for both of us.

She was also relieved that Josh hadn't made anymore of the mysterious remarks that had worried her at the beginning of the semester. *He might have liked me at first,* she decided. *But I was very clear about where I stood. So it's purely a business relationship. Bruce is the only boy in my life.*

"Want some popcorn?" Bruce whispered, leaning close to her in the dark.

Darcy shook her head. "No, thanks."

They relapsed into silence and tried to concentrate on the pitifully bad movie they had come to see.

A few minutes later she tried to talk to him. "Isn't this dumb?"

"Yeah."

Yeah. Yeah, she thought. *This is dumb. Why can't we talk to each other?* Tears welled up in Darcy's eyes, surprising her. She touched Bruce's arm. "You want to leave?"

Crouching over, the two made their way out of the row of seats and hurried up the aisle. They didn't speak again until they had pulled out of the parking lot, and Darcy realized he was headed for Lookout Point.

"Look out," she said with a ghost of a smile. The old joke made Bruce chuckle. But he turned the radio on, and they were silent the rest of the way.

For a while they sat quietly, looking at the lights twinkling in the town below them and thinking their own thoughts. Finally, Darcy sighed, then reached for Bruce's hand in the dark.

"How's your project for Mr. Webb going?"

"OK. But Nancy and I have had a lot of arguments. She's sort of hard to work with."

"I'm not surprised to hear that," she answered with a soft chuckle.

"I'll be glad when this is all over," Bruce said after a short pause.

"Me, too." It was barely a whisper, and Bruce pulled her close.

Darcy looked up into his face in the darkness; he brushed her lips briefly with his own and then pulled away. He sat looking out the window. Darcy's hand clenched involuntarily. Where was the excitement she used to feel whenever he touched her?

Suddenly, without warning, tears began to run unchecked down her face. She cried softly, her face buried in Bruce's shoulder.

"Hey, hey, what's wrong, Darce?"

She shook her head, not knowing what to say.

"Listen, when the semester's over, we'll have the whole summer together. We'll just forget about this whole thing, OK? And start over?"

With a sniff, Darcy lifted her head and tried to read his expression, but it was too dark to see anything except shadow in Bruce's face. She swallowed hard and nodded. "You're right. We'll just forget this whole semester."

But then Josh's face suddenly appeared before her eyes, and she knew the semester could not simply be erased from her mind. It was too late for that.

Chapter Eight

Josh leaned over as the bell rang to end Mr. Webb's social studies class. "I'll meet you at the parking lot after last period, OK?"

"Sure. See you later."

Darcy got up slowly and gathered her books, watching as Josh maneuvered his way through the desks to the door.

"Darcy, you ready?"

She looked over her shoulder and managed a smile. "Sure, Bruce. Let's go."

As she and Bruce entered the chaos of the hallway, Darcy mentally went over everything she had to accomplish that afternoon. She and Josh were going to his house to prepare their final presentation—and that meant working as long and as late as necessary to get the material in shape. They could be picked first or last—they wouldn't know until the next day's class.

"Bruce, I'm getting a ride with Josh this afternoon. We have to do the presentation." She cast a sidelong glance at her boyfriend, who was walking moodily alongside her.

He nodded absently. "Yeah, I know. Me, too."

They continued down the hall, pausing to greet friends and make way for packs of kids. Darcy gripped her books tightly, thinking of how Bruce might have reacted four months ago if she had told him she was riding in another boy's car. She shrugged and heaved a sigh. *Don't even think about it now,* she commanded herself. *You've got too much to worry about this afternoon, with the project looming over you. The semester's almost over, and you can figure out what's going on when school's out. Just think about Bruce later.*

"Talk to you later, Bruce. OK?"

He gave her arm a quick squeeze before turning away. "Yeah. All right. 'Bye."

Two hours later she was hurrying to the parking lot, checking her book bag to see if she had everything she needed.

"Hi," she said breathlessly as she jogged up

to Josh, who stood beside his battered old Volkswagen.

"You in some kind of a hurry?" he said, leaning back against the car.

"I just want to get this over with, OK?"

Josh blinked. "Oh."

"Oh, Josh," Darcy said, pausing as she opened the car door. "I didn't mean it like that, really. I just mean, it's almost finished, after all the work we've done. That's all. You should know by now I never mean what I say."

He shrugged and gave her a wry grin. "No problem. Let's go."

The engine sputtered to life, and they pulled out of the parking lot with a few jolts. "Takes a while for it to warm up," Josh shouted over the noise. "Here we go."

Darcy sat back and looked out the window, feeling that special happiness that only comes with driving away from school.

"I'd better warn you, there's going to be quite a reception committee when we get to my house," Josh was saying.

She turned to him and raised her eyebrows questioningly. "What's that supposed to mean? Or shouldn't I ask?"

With a laugh Josh shook his head. "I tried to make them promise they'd leave you alone, but there's no telling what'll happen. I'm afraid they're dying of curiosity."

"Just who is 'they'?"

"My mom and my little brother."

Darcy grinned. "Beau, the baby Confederate?"

"The very one. He's so excited about meeting my wife, he could hardly get to sleep last night."

"What?" Darcy turned, twisting in her seat so she could face Josh without craning her neck, and folded her arms. "Now what on earth did you tell him that for?"

Josh signaled for a right turn and shot her a quick grin. "Well—I tried to explain to him it's only make-believe stuff. Just pretend. But, well—"

"Josh! He's only three years old! How's he supposed to understand something like that?"

Josh just grinned sheepishly and shrugged.

"Well, I think that's terrible—now he's going to think I'm his real sister-in-law, right?"

"Don't worry. He hasn't gotten that far in his study of interfamily relationships yet."

Darcy shook her head. "You're incorrigible, Josh." But she couldn't help answering his grin with one of her own.

"Just do me a favor, OK?"

Rolling her eyes in mock despair, Darcy groaned. "Now what?"

"Hey, come on! Give me a break. Just go along with it for Beau's sake, OK? It's too confusing to explain."

"Confusing! You're the one who got him confused in the first place!"

"I know. So I thought you'd do the right thing and try not to mix him up anymore. Please?"

Darcy narrowed her eyes and shook her fist in Josh's face. "You're really asking for it, you know?"

He chuckled. "I'll take my chances."

They were silent for a few moments. Darcy shook her head and smiled. Josh had an uncanny knack for putting other people in embarrassing predicaments, such as the time he had told the salesman she wanted to buy that microwave oven, or when he had told Mr. Webb that Darcy thought she could run the class better than he if she had the chance. But it was impossible to get mad at him—he was always so funny.

Darcy sat up as they pulled up to a hand-some brick house. "Is this it?"

He nodded. "Here we are."

As Darcy opened her door, she noticed a small, curly head peeking through a front window. A pair of dark eyes surveyed her solemnly, and she shot Josh a quick look.

"Ever get the feeling you're being watched?" he asked, leading the way up the flagstone path.

She drew a deep breath and hoisted her bag over one shoulder. "Ready or not, here I am."

Josh opened the door and stood back to let her pass. Stepping into the hall, Darcy encountered a small boy with a stuffed toy in one hand. She put her hand out and bent over.

"How do you do? My name is Darcy."

Beau looked past her at Josh, then stuck one finger in his mouth. Darcy glanced back at Josh over her shoulder.

"It's OK, Beau. This is the lady I told you about."

The little boy's eyes opened even wider, and a shy smile appeared on his lips. He put his hand hesitantly in Darcy's, but then pulled it away quickly and hid it behind his back after a brief shake. Then, with small, tentative steps, Beau began inching backward until he was standing behind a chair. From that haven he stared at Darcy.

She fought hard not to laugh. "Is he always such a blabbermouth?"

With a laugh, Josh led the way down the hall. "He's just shy. Give him a little time, and he'll talk your ear off. Here's the kitchen. I thought we could eat something first. If you'd like," he hurried to add, remembering his chivalrous southern manners.

"Yes, I would—thank you." Darcy smiled as a tall, fair-haired woman rose from a table by a plant-filled window and walked toward them. "Hi, I'm Darcy Stevens."

Mrs. Foster took her hand. "I am so delighted to meet you, Darcy," she said, her soft voice made musical by her lilting accent. She beamed at her son. "Josh hasn't stopped talking about you since this semester began. I swear, you've absolutely bewitched him, my dear."

Darcy blushed but was surprised to see Josh merely smile as he kissed his mother's cheek. "Don't you go making up stories, Mama," he chided, his own drawl more noticeable now that he was home.

"Well, now, let's have some iced tea. Would you like that, Darcy? It's full of fresh mint." Mrs. Foster glided to the refrigerator and pulled out a frosty pitcher. She turned to Darcy with an inquisitive smile.

"I'd love some, thank you." Darcy accepted a glass and helped herself from a plate of ginger cookies Mrs. Foster held out. She stood for a moment in the middle of the room, enchanted by the warmth and grace that seemed to emanate from Josh's mother and everything around her. The sunny kitchen was decorated with copper molds and old vegetable-seed envelopes in colorful frames. Blue-and-yellow rag rugs were scattered across the floor, and in one corner was a pile of cartons and blocks, obviously a creation of Beau's.

She felt a faint tug at the hem of her skirt. Looking down, she found Beau staring up at her. She leaned over. "Hi, Beau."

"Hi. Are you really Josh's wife?"

With a look of exasperation at her "husband," Darcy nodded. Josh laughed and sat down at the table. Darcy looked at Beau again. "That's right. Say, is that your building over there?"

She heard the small intake of breath as he gasped with pleasure. A joyous smile lit up his small face. "Do you want to see it?" he whispered, looking hopefully into her eyes.

"Oh, yes—please. Will you show me?" She took his hand and let him lead her to the miniature construction. Soon he was chattering away, breathlessly pointing out all the features of his model. Darcy took small sips of her iced tea and listened to him babble. She could hear Josh and his mother talking at the table behind them.

"Does it have a secret getaway door?" Darcy asked, hiding a smile.

Beau stood back and studied his building for a long moment. Finally he nodded, his curls bobbing. "Yes," he said, crouching down and pointing to a paper-towel tube. "It's in there."

"Will the people be able to get through there?" Darcy continued, peering into the opening. "It's very small."

Beau shook his head anxiously, his dark eyes big in his chubby face. "No! No! It's for mice!"

"Oh, I see." Darcy rocked back on her heels and glanced up as Josh walked over to them. She gave him a lopsided smile.

He grinned. "Beau, do you mind if I take Darcy away now? We have to do some work."

The little boy looked crestfallen. "Homework? For school?"

Darcy laughed and hugged her new friend. "Yes. It's special homework. But I'll come back and play with you later, OK?"

He appeared to be considering the offer. "OK," he decided, "in five minutes."

"That's right, Beau. We'll be back in five minutes." Josh nodded toward the door, and he and Darcy left the kitchen. "He has no conception of time so we always say five minutes. It could be four hours, and he'd never know the difference. It's all the same to him. Come on, my room's down the hall here."

"Josh, your little brother is adorable. I love him." Darcy set her books down on the big desk in Josh's room and looked around her at the oak furniture, bamboo shades, and orange shag rug on the floor. "This is nice."

Josh shrugged. "It's my mom. She does everything."

There was a pause as Darcy and Josh looked at each other. "Well," Darcy said, "shall we get to work?"

"OK, let's go over this again," she said three hours later. "This leaves us forty dollars a week for anything we want."

"Discretionary income," Josh interrupted, trying to balance a pencil on his thumb.

Darcy grabbed the pencil. "Pay attention," she scolded, tapping him on the head with the eraser end before she handed it back.

"Are you sure about the food budget?" Josh asked, briefly scanning the list. "Are we going to have enough left over for baby clothes and a stroller—?"

"Josh, I'm telling you. I asked a million people—my mom, my Aunt Lucy—everyone. And they all agree. If you eat eggs or spaghetti for dinner at least twice a week and shop for cheaper cuts of meat, you can do it." She waited for him to object further, but he didn't. "So what about this forty dollars? Do you want to stick it in the savings account with the rest or go out on the town once a week?"

"Hmm." Josh continued to stare at his pencil, shaking his head. "Look at this," he commanded, holding it out like a piece of evidence.

Darcy looked skeptical. "Very nice, Josh. Now about this money—"

"That's just what I'm talking about. We don't have any room in our budget for pencils."

"Josh, have you just lost your mind? We have until tomorrow to get this ironed out, and I don't think this is really the time to start acting weird. Come on—be serious."

He jumped up and began pacing the floor. "No, listen for a minute. All along I've been worried about something. We had this budget worked out to the last penny—everything was covered. But we never made any allowance for pencils—"

"Josh—"

"Or newspapers, or pay phones, or—"

"Stamps, or birthday presents," Darcy put in as she realized what her partner was driving at.

Josh nodded and sat down again, straddling a chair. "If we put that in our presentation —that we've got forty dollars a week for miscellaneous little things—"

"Webb will be ecstatic."

They grinned at each other. "We're going to ace this one, Darcy. I know it."

For a moment Darcy just sat still, looking down at the pages of charts and notebook paper spread out in front of them. She smiled, shaking her head. "Wow, I'm exhausted." She looked out the window, suddenly aware of the chorus of peepers that had started up while they had been working.

"Would you like to stay for dinner? I know my mother is counting on it."

Darcy looked back at Josh. "Your mother's really nice. I like her."

"She likes you, too. She told me so while you were playing with Beau."

With a quiet laugh, Darcy said, "Well, it's a good thing. Mothers-in-law are supposed to be horrendous."

"You've got nothing to worry about there," Josh said. "My mother has always been like pecan pie—all sugar. And as for Beau, you've really made a conquest there. You'll never be able to get rid of him now."

"Maybe he could be my 'foster' child," she teased, unable to resist the pun.

Josh groaned. "There is no punishment severe enough for that kind of joke."

They smiled at each other again, sharing a sense of companionship and accomplishment. The moment grew longer, but their gazes held. Without a word, Josh leaned over and kissed Darcy's lips.

Instinctively, Darcy responded to his kiss, and her hand went up to touch his cheek. But at the same moment, they both seemed to awaken, as if from a dream, and sprang apart.

Josh was breathing quickly and blushing, and he stumbled over a chair as he backed up. "I—I beg your pardon. I—" He looked around frantically and opened the door. "I'd better take you home now."

Darcy sat frozen for a moment, staring at the chair Josh had been sitting on. Then, she stood up in a daze and gathered her books together. Silently, the two walked through the house to Josh's car and headed for the Stevenses'.

They drove to Darcy's house in shocked silence, neither able to speak at all. When they pulled into the oval driveway, Josh stopped the car and sat looking straight ahead. He cleared his throat with a painful sound.

"I don't know what happened, Darcy. I've known from the beginning—you've made it clear—that you are committed to Bruce, and I should never have done such a thing. And I promise it will never happen again. I—I'm very sorry."

Darcy stared at him, her thoughts whirling. "That's OK," she whispered, not knowing what she meant. Getting out of the car, she added, "See you tomorrow."

With a terse nod, Josh started the engine. Darcy slammed the door and stood watching as he drove away. Then she turned and walked slowly to her house.

Chapter Nine

"OK, now I'll be calling on you at random, so some of you get a little delay in sharing the happy accounts of your 'marriages' with us. But I do want all the budgets and all the written reports turned in at the end of this period." Over the groans, Mr. Webb added, "That way, none of you can sneak in any little tidbits you might have picked up from your fellow 'hubbies' and 'wives.'"

"Now, before we begin, let me put your minds at ease a bit, if I can. Although I think this balmy weather may have already sent your brains on a premature summer vacation."

There was a scattering of whistles and applause before he could go on.

"It's very likely that as you listen to these reports, you'll find that some people did things very differently than you did. You might think your way is either better or worse.

"But listen." He paced back and forth in front of his students, his arms swinging wildly as he emphasized his words. "There is no one correct way to live. Right? You go out into the world, and you test the water. Then you make your decisions. I intend to respect each of your decisions, whether they seem profitable or practical, or even if they would in reality be unwise in the long run. As long as I think they are well-considered decisions, I will accept them." Drawing a deep breath, he shrugged. "So, any questions before we hear the first report?"

No one spoke. Darcy felt as though all the kids were holding their breaths, waiting to find out who would be called on first. No one had any energy to spare to think of questions.

Mr. Webb scanned the list in his hand and looked up. "So, without further ado—Susan and Chuck, let's hear your story."

Chairs scraped as the students sat back to listen. There was more than a little relief on everyone else's part—relief that they wouldn't have to go first.

Susan Olsen and Chuck Weinberg looked momentarily taken aback. But they exchanged a brief smile and a thumbs-up sign as they walked up to the front of the room, sat down at the table there, and prepared to face the class.

"Well, before we begin," Susan announced, opening a notebook, "I'll have to tell you that our presentation is going to be very different from all the others."

"Go on," prodded Mr. Webb as she paused. "We're all ears."

Chuck pulled on his jaw, then gave a short laugh. "Well, we ah—had a few differences of opinion when we started out—and Susan said she wanted to get a divorce." He halted for a moment until the laughter subsided. "So what we decided to do, actually, was, well, we decided to get divorced."

For a shocked moment no one said a word. Darcy looked quickly at Mr. Webb, and so did almost everyone else. He sat very still, his gaze shifting from Susan to Chuck and back again. It began to look as though he might object, and the two up front were becoming visibly worried.

But a faint smile appeared on his face, and it soon turned into a broad grin, and then a laugh. "OK, good enough!" he cried, striking the desk in front of him with his palm. "OK, let's hear what divorce is all about, you cynics."

Audible sighs of relief escaped from Susan

and Chuck. But the two immediately got down to business.

"First of all, we called some lawyers and legal-aid services—to see how expensive it would be—"

"How about going to Reno?" someone suggested.

Susan pushed on. "How expensive it would be here—"

"Yeah," Chuck cut in, leaning forward eagerly. "And it really varies. Like if you have kids, it can be a total hassle. But, fortunately, we don't," he added, sending his teacher a grin.

"Good, good." Mr. Webb smiled, nodding happily.

"And then we had to figure out joint property. Which we didn't have—"

"But we decided to get some property first —to go through the procedures. And then split it . . ."

As the two outlined the course they had followed all semester, Darcy gave only half her attention to their story, even though it was really entertaining. Her thoughts had been in a tailspin since the previous evening, when Josh had dropped her off and sped away. And for once in her life, plain-spoken, straightforward Darcy Stevens was at a total loss.

She stole a peek at Josh out of the corner of her eye. His greeting that day had bordered on the cold, to say the least. A curt nod and a "hello" before turning away was all he had given her. There was no smile, none of his easy southern charm.

But for her part, Darcy couldn't even remember if she had given him much more. She realized with a grimace that she had most likely turned beet red and stammered "hi"—or something equally unsophisticated. All she knew for sure was that at the time, she had been standing very close to Bruce, as if for protection.

Darcy shook her head miserably. *What is going on here?* she wanted to scream. *I didn't want him to kiss me! Or did I?* All she knew was that now, instead of the easy camaraderie she and Josh used to share, there was an awkward, nerve-racking tension in the air between them.

"So when we finally got down to it, we both started looking for lawyers," Susan was saying, pulling some yellow sheets from her folder. "So we looked in the Yellow Pages—and can you believe this? Eight pages of attorneys!"

This was greeted by laughter from the class. Darcy managed a thin smile and tried to pay attention during the rest of the talk. Their

127

presentation finally concluded, Chuck and Susan returned to their seats amid laughter and applause.

"Very nice, you two. But you took quite a chance pulling a stunt like that." Mr. Webb stood up and swung his arms as he strode to the front of the class. "But I'm glad you did," he continued. "Because it shows that you picked up one of my most important lessons. If nothing else, I want you to be bold, enterprising, creative, and above all, to take risks. That is the only way to learn!" he shouted, pounding the table for emphasis.

He paused, surprised by his own energy, and beamed at the class. "So, let's have another one. Darcy and Josh, are you ready?"

Darcy looked up, startled, to meet Mr. Webb's intense gaze. Hardly daring to look at her partner, she nodded. "Yeah, I guess so."

"Yes, sir, we're ready," came Josh's clear, strong voice.

Darcy turned to meet his eyes, afraid of what she might see. But he looked at her steadily, his fascinating blue-brown eyes holding no message at all. "After you," he said with a trace of his old humor.

Nervously gathering her materials, Darcy stood and preceded Josh to the front of the room. She was excruciatingly conscious of him walking behind her, and she felt relieved when they sat down. She looked across the room at Bruce, who smiled supportively.

She drew a deep breath. "Here we go," she muttered before launching into her opening remarks.

As Darcy spoke, she was only too aware of Josh sitting beside her, listening intently to what she said. That awareness made her acutely uncomfortable, and she stammered and stumbled through her words. Once she suddenly lost track of where she was, and she thought she could sense a look of growing disappointment on Mr. Webb's face.

"And so our initial goal was to get ourselves started with only ten thousand dollars of our savings," she concluded unhappily a few minutes later.

Josh picked up his cue there. "So we managed to find an apartment we could afford on our combined salaries, and we set out to furnish it for five thousand dollars." He broke off, looking down at his list. He looked quickly at Darcy, his expression unreadable. Then, flashing her a grin, he went on, "We weren't going to tell you about this part, but for some reason I feel I've got to fill you in on how we spent this vast sum of money the first time around."

Darcy's eyes widened. "Josh, come on. Let's not get into that, OK?"

"Why not?"

"Because. It—it's too embarrassing!" she stammered, her voice failing her from sheer nervousness.

"Darcy! Hold the phone—hold the phone!" interjected Mr. Webb, smiling gleefully and rubbing his hands together. "Are you trying to deprive us of a good story?"

A rousing chorus of support for Josh brought the color out on Darcy's cheeks. She bit her lower lip in consternation. "But, Mr. Webb, we changed it all, so it isn't even part of our report. I mean, it'll only be a waste of time."

"Now, I'll be the judge of that. Making mistakes is part of the game here. Let's hear it, Josh."

"Yes, sir."

As Josh forged ahead and told the class how their first impulse had been to buy all the luxury items in sight—the stereo, the microwave, the water bed—Darcy wished she could have sunk through the scuffed linoleum floor and disappeared into the ground. Why was he telling that dumb story? Was he deliberately trying to make her feel bad? Was he angry with her about yesterday? What exactly did he want?

But as he continued talking, she realized it wasn't really all that embarrassing—at least, not the way he told it. And it didn't make her feel bad at all. It was actually pretty funny. And apparently everyone else thought so, too. Soon the whole class was in stitches, and Darcy was laughing as hard as the rest. Josh remained perfectly straight-faced and sober through the telling and even managed to look surprised that everyone was laughing.

"That was when we decided to buy the 'dishwasher-safe, impact-resistant plastic dinnerware' instead of the china," he concluded, his eyes shining. "And we saved quite a lot by doing it, let me tell you. Only problem is, it makes your food taste like an old air mattress."

Darcy leaned back, smiling. "Well, now that that's over with," she said in a mock-scolding tone, "can we please get on with it?"

For the next twenty minutes, she and Josh delivered the rest of their presentation without a hitch. Their careful preparation paid off with both of them explaining different facets of their program. Darcy forced herself to put aside her turbulent emotions and concentrate on her work, and after a while she didn't even have to try.

She outlined how they had picked their apartment and the terms of their lease. Then she went on to describe the different bank accounts they had, and how they had arrived at some of the figures in their budget.

Next, Josh detailed the purchases they had needed to make for their baby, then discussed the process of getting a car loan and buying insurance for their new "previously owned vehicle."

"Although I still think we could have used my old VW," he complained, casting an imploring look at Mr. Webb.

"No way. From scratch, as I said."

Josh made a slight bow from his chair. "As you said. Anyway, when the baby came along, we got more insurance," He grinned at Darcy: it had been a hotly contested issue.

"Yeah," she joined in, shaking her head at the memory. "We each took out a life insurance policy. Ten thousand dollars."

"*Ooo-hoo!* A very nice touch." Mr. Webb applauded. "And always a nice motive for murder."

Darcy laughed along with the rest of the class. "Don't think it hasn't already crossed our minds!"

"Yeah, but who's going to kill whom?" called out one student.

Josh leaned forward. "I think that's obvious, don't you?" He edged his chair away from Darcy. "I'm terrified of her."

Catcalls and whistles sounded out from the boys in the class, and Darcy couldn't help grinning at her partner. He smiled back, and they finished up the report. As she came to the end, Darcy couldn't help feeling a spark of triumph as she delivered the punch line. "And we now have six thousand five hundred eighty-nine dollars and seventy-two cents in our savings account." *Toward our trip around the world,* she added silently.

Mr. Webb nodded. "Not bad, not bad."

"Not bad!" Darcy wailed. "Oh, Mr. Webb, don't you think it was better than that?"

"OK, OK! It was terrific, you two. Congratulations."

Folding up her notes, Darcy began to rise, but Mr. Webb halted her.

"Hold on, we're not quite through yet." He folded his arms and surveyed his students. "Let's hear some comments from some of you. For instance, what in particular did Darcy and Josh do that you didn't, but that you would do if you could add it in before the end of the class when you have to turn in your reports?"

"The pencil-and-newspaper fund."

"Having a separate account for paying income tax."

Barbie Scoffield raised her hand. "I think it was really smart the way they didn't try to get the best of everything. I mean, they were really practical and conservative, so they were able to afford everything they needed. There was a lot of stuff we didn't get, because it didn't fit our budget after we bought more expensive things."

Restraining a laugh, Darcy nodded. "Well, it took a lot of trial and error to get there, you know." She paused, remembering her first meeting with Josh, when she had insisted on buying a house in the most expensive part of town. The memory of their first wild shopping spree came back, too, along with a dozen other vivid scenes of the semester-long project. "My partner," she continued, her voice heavy with sarcasm, "was able to convince me of the 'merits of economy.' Or, in other words, half the time he just flat out refused to go along with my ideas!"

From the smiles in her audience, Darcy could tell she'd struck a familiar note. She shrugged and turned to Josh. "I guess we're done."

"Yes, we certainly are." Josh turned away from her abruptly and handed one copy of their report to Mr. Webb. Then he got up and walked back to his seat.

Darcy followed more slowly, feeling that a burden had been lifted from her shoulders. Or was it more of a feeling of loss? She really wasn't sure.

The bell rang moments later, and Josh turned to her as their classmates surged to the front of the room to turn in their reports.

"Well, now that it's over, I'll keep out of your way," he said, looking past her rather than at her. "Thank you for being such a good partner." On that note, he turned and strode from the room.

Darcy stood openmouthed, staring at his retreating figure, until he turned into the hallway outside and disappeared. Her chest felt tight, and she swallowed hard. Was that it? Was it all over? She suddenly couldn't believe that she wouldn't be meeting Josh in the library anymore, wouldn't be talking to him on the phone and discussing their project before class. It was all over.

"You're welcome," she whispered, her voice no more than a faint breath.

"Ready to go?"

She turned and looked up into Bruce's eyes. "Sure, I guess so."

As Bruce draped one arm across her shoulders, she felt a twinge of regret. *Well, I guess it's back to normal now,* she thought, conscious of Bruce's touch. *That's what I've been waiting for all semester, after all. As for the rest*—she sighed—*it was only make-believe.*

Chapter Ten

Darcy stood in front of her mirror, absently brushing her hair as she listened to the soft evening noises outside her window. Birds twittered to one another sleepily as they settled in for the night; a chorus of peepers started up. In the distance, she could hear two kids call out to each other as they rode their bikes home from the park.

She glanced at the clock—quarter of eight, and still so light out. Putting aside her brush, Darcy walked to the window seat and sat down, resting her chin in one hand. For several minutes she stayed that way, letting her mind wander as she took in the twilight.

The crunch of tires on gravel and a sweep of headlights across her ceiling told Darcy that Bruce had arrived. She snatched a light jacket from the closet and ran downstairs to meet him. It was back to normal with Bruce, just as she had been wishing it would be all spring. They had been going out a few nights a week since summer vacation started; it was a habit, really.

She found him talking to her parents in the kitchen, and after a few minutes of small talk, they left the house.

"How about a movie?" Bruce asked as they headed for the downtown area.

"Sure, anything. I don't care." *I don't care*, Darcy repeated to herself. *I really don't.* She glanced at Bruce's face, lit by oncoming traffic, and shook her head. Things were back to normal on the surface, maybe. But underneath, nothing was the same.

"Why don't we just go to the mall—let's check out who's there?" she suggested, wanting to see other people, new faces.

He shrugged. "OK." He made a left-hand turn, and soon they were driving down the long thoroughfare to the huge shopping center and looking for a parking spot.

"Let's go to O'Henry's," Darcy decided, reaching for Bruce's hand as they walked toward the brilliantly lit mall. "I feel like ice cream tonight."

"Good idea."

Darcy glanced at Bruce again. *What would Josh have said to that?* she asked herself. *Probably something corny like "Funny, you don't look like ice cream."* Corny maybe, but she would rather hear that than just "Good idea." She hated to admit it, but sometimes Bruce was a little dull. There. She had come right out and said it to herself, for the first time. Bruce wasn't as bright and witty and interesting as she wished he were—not nearly so much as Josh was, for instance.

But you have to live with other people's shortcomings, a little voice scolded. *Not everyone is perfect.* Not Bruce, not you, and not Josh Foster. Most definitely not Josh Foster—he puts you in embarrassing situations, and you can never tell when he's serious.

"Oh, forget it," she said out loud.

"Huh?"

She jumped, surprised that she had spoken. "Oh, nothing, just talking to myself," she explained with a guilty smile. Bruce smiled back, and a new wave of guilt washed over Darcy. *I can't imagine not being Bruce's girlfriend,* she realized. *He's been a part of my life for so long.*

As they entered the cavernous space of the mall, they paused to get their bearings. "There are so many entrances to this thing, I never

139

know where I am," Darcy chattered, suddenly feeling nervous and jittery as they joined the milling stream of Friday-night mall-goers. "It's so confusing. They ought to have one door. Period. That way you would never get lost."

Bruce shrugged. "I don't think they would do that. It doesn't really make sense."

"Well, everything doesn't always have to make sense, does it?" Darcy flashed, angry for no reason at all.

He frowned. "Come on, let's get some ice cream."

Moving forward through the crowd, Darcy looked around her. Tall, light-seeking trees grew upward through the vast structure, reaching for the huge skylights above. From the second level, a waterfall splashed down into a poolful of coins tossed in for wishes. As she craned her neck to look up, she noticed a department store sign—their department store. She flushed as she remembered the riotous scene she and Josh had played out there, and when they'd collapsed on the sofa, convulsed with laughter after having thrown the drab little microwave-oven salesman into utter confusion by having claimed to be married.

A heady chocolate scent pulled her attention forward again; they had reached their favorite ice-cream joint, O'Henry's, and it was mobbed.

"We'll never get a booth," she said, looking anxiously into the packed space.

Bruce stood up on his toes to see over the heads of the people waiting for takeout orders. "Hey, there's Josh Foster and a little kid at a booth. Maybe he'll let us sit with them."

Darcy's heart leaped into her mouth. "But, Bruce, I—"

Before Darcy could protest, Bruce led her forward and around the counters to where Josh and Beau Foster sat.

"Hi, Josh, how's it going?" Bruce said, sliding into the booth without looking at either Darcy or Josh.

"Darcy!" The ecstatic voice belonged to Beau, whose fudge-smeared little face lit up when he saw her.

"Come on, Beau, shove over. There's plenty of room," Josh offered, sliding over to make room for Bruce and gazing up at Darcy, his face the expressionless mask she had seen so often.

She hesitated, but Beau was beginning to climb up on the seat to grab her arm, so she sat down, trying to look anywhere but at Josh. Beau made that easy enough.

"Look what I got!" he commanded, pushing his sundae toward her.

"It looks great. Hot fudge, carmel, marsh-mallow. What kind of ice cream is it?"

He spooned an adult-sized bite of sundae into his small mouth. " 'Nilla," he managed to choke out, "an' maple walnut."

Darcy had to laugh, and she turned to Josh with a smile in spite of herself. "I've heard you southerners like things sweet," she said, reaching for a menu.

"Don't let him fool you. We're turning into real Yanks these days."

"And just what is that supposed to mean?"

"When we aren't here eating ice cream, we eat raw cranberries and pumpkin pie. And salted cod. Real Puritan stuff. *Yumm-mee.*"

"Oh, come on, Josh." She laughed. "That's going a little too far. Mocha chip with malt, please—in a dish," she ordered as the wait-ress paused by their booth, pencil in hand.

"Talk about sweet," she heard Josh murmur.

"I'll have a banana supreme with straw-berry ice cream," Bruce declared, handing the menu back to the waitress. He turned to Josh. "So, what are you doing for the sum-mer? Baby-sitting?"

Josh took Bruce's probing with a polite smile. "Some of that, some of this. Actually, I'm doing a lot of house painting."

"Oh, yeah? I did that last summer with this guy . . ."

The two boys continued talking, and Darcy sat back, picking at her ice cream half-heartedly. Beau kept up a constant monologue about his day-camp activities, and she was able to keep him happy by smiling and nodding a lot.

From time to time she glanced across the table at Josh, watching him talk. His eyes were striking in his tanned face, and he spoke in that relaxed way of his that made getting along with him so easy.

Suddenly, as she looked at him, she remembered with a pang of regret that she was with Bruce, not him. Before long she would have to say good-bye to Josh and Beau, and she and Bruce would leave together. *I want to leave with Josh,* she realized. Her eyes widened with the sudden revelation. *I don't love Bruce at all, anymore. I'm in love with Josh Foster.*

Her heart pounding in her chest, Darcy looked down at her quickly melting dish of ice cream. Elation and despair battled for control of her emotions as she gradually came to accept what she had been denying for so long. *I love Josh. I love Josh. Not Bruce. Not at all.*

"Darcy?"

She looked up, her eyes stinging from the threat of tears. Josh and Beau were standing. "Are you leaving?" she asked, her voice hoarse.

Beau nodded sadly. Then he brightened. "Do you ever go to the pool? Maybe you'll see me there. Josh takes me a lot, don't you?" he added, looking up lovingly into his big brother's face.

Josh ruffled Beau's hair. "That's right, Mr. Potato-Head." he looked at Darcy and Bruce again. "Hope you guys have a good summer. And if I don't run into you again, I'll see you at school in September."

Darcy nodded mutely. "Sure," Bruce said, spooning up the last of his sundae. "See you around. He's an OK guy, you know?" he continued, as Josh and Beau disappeared into the crowd. "His little brother's a cute kid."

"Yeah, he is." Darcy stared down at her hands. She was surprised to see that she had been systematically tearing a paper napkin to shreds. With a cry of disgust, she balled up the pieces and threw them down. "Let's go. Are you ready?"

Bruce took a long swallow of water and nodded. "Sure, let me just pay for this."

Now the glitter and activity of the mall seemed harsh to Darcy, and she steered a course straight for the exit. If Bruce noticed her haste, he didn't object. It was only when they reached the reflecting pool that he pulled up short.

"Hey, hold on a second. I want to make a wish."

Darcy smiled sadly. "Sure. What's your wish?"

"If I tell, it won't come true," he reminded her, looking into her eyes. She turned away as he dug in his pocket for a coin. "Here goes." The dime flipped up, flashing as it turned, and then plummeted into the water. They watched it rock from side to side as it sank gracefully to the bottom, where it rested among the pennies, nickels, dimes, and quarters.

"I'm going to make a wish, too," Darcy declared, fishing a shiny new penny out of her purse. As she let it fall into the shimmering pool, she thought, *I wish—I wish to be happy. And I can't be with you, Bruce. I know that now.* Darcy stared into the water at the glittering coins. *I can't stay with you. Mom was right. I have to listen to my heart.*

As they left the pool and approached the long flank of doors to the parking lot, Darcy put her hand on Bruce's arm to stop him. "Let's go up to Lookout Point, all right?"

He looked searchingly into her eyes; he seemed to be almost as troubled as she was. There was a long moment of silence. Then he nodded. "Sure."

They were silent on the drive up to the point. Darcy was trying hard to control her emotions, and she didn't dare speak. What she had to say to Bruce was going to be the hardest thing she had ever had to face.

Bruce pulled up into the Lookout Point parking lot and rolled down his window as he stopped the car. The sudden stillness made their lack of communication even more acute.

"Bruce—"

"Wait—wait, let's just sit here for a minute, OK?"

Drawing a shaky breath, Darcy nodded. She sat back and stared out the window, feeling the cool, moist air flow gently past her face. A breeze picked up, carrying the scent of rain and stirring the leaves of the trees behind them. She put her hand out the window and felt the first few sprinkling drops. As the rain intensified, her hand quickly became wet, and she pulled it in, drawing her jacket around her shoulders.

"Bruce, I—I think I want to . . ." Darcy's voice trailed off. She was unable to say the words.

Bruce took her hand in the dark. "What are you trying to say, Darce?" His voice was low, and Darcy thought he might be trying not to cry.

That thought released the tears she had been holding back, and she began to cry softly, her hands over her face as the rain pattered quietly on the roof of the car. Bruce sighed and pulled her to him; he caressed her hair. "Do you want to break up, Darcy? Is that it?"

She nodded, still powerless to speak.

For a while they sat that way, neither of them speaking. But ironically, Darcy felt closer to Bruce than she had in months. Maybe that's what telling the truth does, she thought, wiping her nose with a tissue. She cherished for the last time the feel of Bruce's arm around her. Then she sat up straight.

"Do you understand, Bruce? It just—it hasn't been right for a long time, and I—"

He nodded. "I guess I knew it, too. But I didn't want to admit it, you know?" He looked into her eyes with a tender smile. "I guess it was hard to imagine not having you around. It's been a long time."

Darcy smiled, though the tears still welled up in her eyes. "I know, Bruce. And I'll always remember how great it was. I'll always love you—as a good, good friend."

He touched her cheek softly and then kissed her forehead. "Me, too." He sighed. "I think I better take you home now."

"Yeah. I think that's probably a good idea."

Darcy tightened her grip on her beach bag and looked across the wide lawn surrounding the pool. It was a typical hot July day, and the park was mobbed. She pushed her sunglasses up on her nose and walked forward, feeling embarrassed, foolish, and excited all at the same time.

"Here goes," she murmured under her breath.

"What?" Sandra asked, meeting her at the gate. She stepped back and looked Darcy up and down. "Are you high on something, Darcy?"

Darcy shook her head with a laugh. "Don't be a dope. Come on."

They found a clear spot on the grass and spread out their beach towels. "I'm going in right now," Sandra declared, pulling her

T-shirt over her head. "You can stay here and roast if you want to."

Nodding slowly, Darcy took her portable cassette player and earphones out of the bag and sat down to wait. She didn't know if it would be that day, the next, or next week. But she had been going to the pool every day for a week. And sooner or later, Josh Foster was bound to show up, little brother in tow.

Lifeguards blew their whistles shrilly, commanding, "Walk, please," to packs of exuberant kids. The diving board pounded and vibrated, as one leap or dive after another was launched from it. Darcy felt almost hypnotized by the broiling sun on her skin, the smell of hot grass, suntan lotion, and chlorine, and the constant flow of action before her eyes. She stretched luxuriantly.

"Darcy! Hey, Darcy, it's me!"

Nearly jumping out of her skin, Darcy turned to see Beau Foster come running toward her. But almost as if he had suddenly remembered his gentlemanly training, he slowed to a dignified walk. It was too bad that that dignity was spoiled by a blue-spotted, inflated sea monster around his chubby waist. Darcy laughed when she saw the little boy, but her eyes quickly went past him.

Josh strolled up just after Beau had dropped

himself down firmly onto Darcy's towel and started his usual running monologue.

"Hi," Darcy said, trying to sound casual. She shielded her eyes as she looked up at him; the sun was right behind his head, throwing his whole face into shadow.

"Nice day. Are you alone?" Josh's voice was as casual as hers, but she suspected—or did she just hope—there was something more there?

She cast a quick glance at Beau, who was blissfully ignorant of the tension in the air.

"No"—she gestured vaguely toward the pool—"Sandra's in there somewhere." Josh made no answer, and she still couldn't see his face.

"Hello?" she said, beginning to feel nervous again. "Anybody there?"

"Oh, sorry. May I sit with you?"

"Of course you can," Beau piped up, pulling on his brother's leg. "It's OK with Darcy, right?"

She nodded. "Yes, of course." Now that he was out of the glare, she could see his face, but she looked away quickly, suddenly shy. "This place is a mob scene today. Look at it. You can barely get in the water—it's wall-to-wall bodies."

"It sure is."

Darcy wanted to scream. *How do you tell someone you broke up with your boyfriend because you're in love with him?* "So, what's new?"

"Nothing much. Just working, mostly. What's new with you?"

"I broke up with Bruce." There, she had said it. But she couldn't believe it. Darcy gulped, afraid to look Josh in the face.

At that moment, Sandra jogged up, dripping wet and wringing water from her hair. "The water feels so good! Hi, Josh," she added, looking with avid curiosity from Darcy to Josh and back again.

"Hi, Sandra. This is my little brother, Beau."

"Hi, Beau. I'm Sandra."

Beau looked up from a pile of grass he'd been busily picking. "Can you dive?"

"Sure." Sandra looked down at Darcy; their eyes met and held for a brief moment. Sandra understood. She held out her hand to Beau. "I can do a back flip. Want to see me? You can sit on the bench and watch."

He stood up willingly. "Yes, please. Can I, Josh?" he pleaded, turning huge eyes to his brother.

"Sure. Stay away from the edge, though. I'll be watching you."

Darcy watched Sandra and Beau walk to

the deep end of the pool. Finally she looked at Josh.

"So," he said, raising his eyebrows. "I guess that means you'll be looking for someone to go fishing with."

"What? I don't know how to fish." Darcy laughed, shaking her head.

He shrugged. "Would you like to try?" he suggested, his southern drawl sounding more pronounced. "I know a fine place."

"What I need is a fine teacher."

"I know one of those, too."

Darcy tucked her knees up under her chin, resisting the impulse to reach over and hug him. "Do I know him?"

"Hmm, probably not. He's this ol' fella—"

But Darcy cut him off by leaning forward and giving him a lingering kiss. She pulled away and laughed breathlessly. "I guess you must think I'm a pretty loose woman," she said, sitting back on her heels.

Josh's fingers went to his mouth, lightly touching the spot where she had kissed him. A slow smile crossed his face. "Well, I'd always heard Yankee girls were—"

"Don't say it!"

"How about if I say something else?"

Darcy pressed her trembling lips together and nodded. "Like what?"

"How about something like, I think I'm in love with you, Darcy Stevens?"

"But you're supposed to be, aren't you?" asked Beau, suddenly appearing before them. "You're supposed to love each other if you're married."

Darcy and Josh both laughed. "That was only make-believe, Beau. Honest," Darcy assured him. "But being in love is not."

We hope you enjoyed reading this book. All the titles currently available in the Sweet Dreams series are listed at the front of the book. They are all available at your local bookshop or newsagent, though should you find any difficulty in obtaining the books you would like, you can order direct from the publisher, at the address below. Also, if you would like to know more about the series, or would simply like to tell us what you think of the series, write to:

Kim Prior
Sweet Dreams
Transworld Publishers Ltd.
61–63 Uxbridge Road
Ealing
London W5 5SA

To order books, please list the title(s) you would like, and send together with a cheque or postal order made payable to TRANS-WORLD PUBLISHERS LTD. Please allow the cost of the book(s) plus postage and packing charges as follows:

All orders up to a total of £5.00: 50p
All orders in excess of £5.00: Free

Please note that payment must be made in pounds sterling; other currencies are unacceptable.

(The above applies to readers in the UK and Republic of Ireland only)

If you live in Australia or New Zealand and would like more information about the series, please write to:

Sally Porter
Sweet Dreams
Transworld Publishers (Aust)
Pty Ltd.
15-23 Helles Avenue
Moorebank
N.S.W. 2170
AUSTRALIA

Kiri Martin
Sweet Dreams
c/o Corgi and Bantam Books
New Zealand
Cnr. Moselle and Waipareira
Avenues
Henderson
Auckland
NEW ZEALAND